TRICKS FOR KICKS

A collection of twenty erotic stories

Edited by Elizabeth Coldwell

Published by Xcite Books Ltd – 2012

ISBN 9781908086563

Copyright © Xcite Books Ltd 2012

Printed and bound by CPI Group (UK) Ltd, Croydon, CR0 4YY

Front cover design by Madamadari

Full cover by Sarah Ann Davies

Contents

Making Her Pay	Veronica Wilde	1
Soul of Discretion	Mary Borsellino	13
Filthy White Dress	Fulani	20
The Best Handjob in the North	Victoria Blisse	31
Mean	Maxim Jakubowski	43
Party Favour	Catelyn Cash	54
Creamed	Landon Dixon	67
I Am Matilda Jenks	Tabitha Rayne	75
Discretion Required	Heidi Champa	83
Airtight	Dominic Santi	92
Perks of the Job	Kay Jaybee	99
Passage to Paradise	Kathleen Tudor	110
Coming While Going …	Marlene Yong	119
Show No Mercy	Giselle Renarde	126
A Discreet Companion	Cecilia Duvalle	138
Shaming Mrs Sloan	Alanna Appleton	150
Myron's Reward	Cynthia Lucas	163
The Third Party	Sommer Marsden	171
Black Swan	Scarlett Blue	182
Three's the Charm	Elizabeth Coldwell	193

Making Her Pay
by Veronica Wilde

The rhythmic thump of the flat tyre began in the darkest, most deserted stretch of the trip. 'No,' Nadia said through gritted teeth. 'No, no, *please* not a flat tyre.' She was driving from Sacramento to Lake Tahoe, a trip she'd made several times, but this part of the highway was miles from anywhere, winding past dark woods that went on for ever. The very worst place to have a flat.

Thump, thump, thud. She pulled over.

'Dammit!' she swore, slamming the ball of her hand on the steering wheel. It wasn't just the busted tyre she was cursing; it was herself, for not replacing the broken spare tyre months ago. Now she'd have to be towed to a local garage, if any were still open this late at night. Or if any garages even existed out here. Once again, she cursed her boss for keeping her so late tonight at the office. On any other Friday night, she would have been with her friends hours ago at the Lake Tahoe house they'd rented. Instead her boss had dumped a pile of work on her desk just before five o'clock, pleading it was an emergency, and she hadn't escaped until well after seven.

Oh well. No use fuming now. Nadia killed the engine and climbed out of the car. The night insect noises of the woods closed over her, reminding her of how utterly deserted this stretch of road was. She inspected her right front flat: hopelessly deflated. With a grimace, she pulled out her road service membership card and cell phone from her purse.

'I've got a flat,' she told the service switchboard. 'And no spare tyre.' She recited her membership number, and gave her location as best she could.

An hour later she was riding through the darkness in a tow truck, listening to more bad news. 'There's a garage five miles ahead,' the driver said. 'But I doubt he's open this late. You really should have fixed your spare.'

'I know,' she said shortly. Didn't the driver realise what an idiot she felt like? How embarrassed and miserable she felt, riding in a tow truck in the middle of nowhere, without any realistic solution in sight? She knew she could call one of her friends at Tahoe to come pick her up, but that was a long trip, and no one would want to leave the Friday night festivities to come rescue her, then bring her back again to pick up the fixed car tomorrow.

They passed a rest stop, then drove past more dark woods. At last lights glimmered ahead, and her heart lifted. That was definitely a garage on the hill, and it looked like it was still open. Thank God. She'd pay anything at this point just to get a new tyre and be on her way. She glanced down at the grey skirt and white silk blouse she'd worn to the office. Not the sexiest outfit, unfortunately, but she could still try to flirt her way into softening up the mechanic. Hopefully it would be some old guy thrilled to have a pretty 25-year-old show some leg. She loosened her long auburn hair from its ponytail and put on lip gloss.

The tow truck pulled up the sloping entrance to the garage. The door opened and a young man in a black T-shirt and jeans walked out, waving both arms in a "go away" gesture. 'We're closed,' he yelled.

The tow truck driver leant out the window. 'She's kind of stuck,' he called back.

Nadia jumped out the passenger side in desperation. 'Please,' she said. 'All I need is a tyre so I can get to Lake Tahoe tonight. I don't have a spare and I don't have anyone who can come get me. Please, I'm begging you. It won't take ten minutes and I'm willing to pay extra.'

The young mechanic's lips lifted in a smile. She tried to contain her booming heart as she studied him. Short blond hair, full lips, and indolent blue eyes: this was no grizzled old mechanic who'd be eager to peep down her blouse. This guy was around her age, and way too cute to be desperate. A cocky grin crept over his face as he openly studied her legs in their black high heels, then the shape of her breasts under the blouse. Clearly he wasn't afraid to check her out and refuse to help her at the same time. Great. Arrogant and cute, the combination least likely to help her.

'Please,' she repeated. 'I'll do anything.'

The words surprised even her. She'd meant to say "pay anything". But now that she was standing here in the cool night, her skirt blowing around her legs, she felt as if she were on an auction block, offering herself up and not just her wallet.

'OK,' he said finally. 'I guess I can spare 15 minutes.'

He jerked his chin at the tow truck driver, who began to unload her car. While the mechanic inspected it, Nadia sighed deeply with relief. This was humiliating, but at least she was getting what she wanted – a new tyre and her continued journey to Lake Tahoe.

As they got the car into the garage, she checked out the way the mechanic's firm ass filled his jeans. He grinned at her over his shoulder and she quickly lifted her eyes. 'I'm Luke,' he said.

'Nadia. Thanks so much for doing this.'

A crooked smile played over his face. He waved goodbye to the tow truck, then gestured to a towering wall of stacked tyres. She wasn't sure how the top rows were accessible until she saw the long ladder anchored to a track on the ceiling and floor. 'Let's see what we've got here,' Luke said. 'Who knows, you could be stuck here all night.'

She didn't entirely like his dirty grin when he said that. But she definitely liked the way he scaled the ladder, that sculpted bottom of his moving rhythmically up the rungs. He found the right tyre and returned with nimble ease to the floor. Then he leant against her car, resting the tyre on the cement floor of the garage.

'So,' he said. 'Let's talk payment.'

Her mouth went dry but she maintained a cool expression. 'Right. How much is the tyre?'

His blond eyebrows lifted. 'The tyre? I was referring to payment for making me stay late on a Friday night to help you out. I mean, I was just locking up and ready to head out. Had all kinds of plans. But –' He shrugged. 'Here I am, helping you. Missing out. So I'm thinking maybe you'll make it up to me.'

Smartass, she thought. But his meaning was clear and the insolent smirk in his blue eyes as he lounged against her car made her nipples tighten.

'Well, of course,' she said. 'Like I said, I'll do anything.' There it was again. *Do* anything.

He picked up a towel and cleaned his hands off. 'Anything?' His languid eyes ran up and down her body.

She felt her cheeks flush. She'd never expected to find herself in this position, offering herself up in return for a favour – and she'd certainly never expected it to feel so thrillingly, nervously exciting. 'Yes … anything.'

His eyes drifted up from her black high heels all the way to her face. 'I don't know,' he said. 'I've already got enough money.'

Her throat was so tight she could barely get the words out. 'I wasn't offering money.'

He stepped up close to her, making her shiver. 'Then let's see what you are offering.'

Oh God. This was really going to happen. She thought for sure Luke would stop, find an excuse to back down, but instead he unbuttoned her white silk top. His fingers deftly undid the material until both sides fell back from her pink lace bra. Luke lightly traced the stiff points of her nipples

4

through the lace, until they were hard and aching. Without taking his eyes from her swelling breasts, he pulled down the cups of her bra until her entire breasts were exposed.

'Nice.' He pulled lightly on each light pink nipple until she bit her lip with desire.

It was all she could do to stand still as he inspected her tits, cupping and squeezing them softly. He stepped up even closer, close enough to kiss her, and she felt his light breath on her neck as he reached around her – and unzipped her skirt. He tugged it down her hips with insistent force until it fell to the garage floor. She took a deep breath as he studied her skimpy black thong.

'Your panties don't match your bra,' he said.

It was a silly thing to be embarrassed by, but she was. 'I was at work,' she said. 'I didn't think anyone was going to see my underwear.'

'Or that you'd get a flat and pay for it by letting a stranger take your clothes off?'

Her annoyance was clearly visible and he laughed.

'Hey, listen,' he said. 'You could have granny panties on for all I could care. Since -' he slipped his hand between her legs and stroked her through the silk '- they're coming off.'

Her skin burned hot. She couldn't believe she was really doing this, letting a strange mechanic strip her naked in a garage with oil-stained concrete, surrounded by auto parts and tyres. Yet there was no denying that Luke knew exactly where to tickle and tease her as his fingers played with her pussy. She opened her thighs with a soft moan, desperate for him to keep touching her. Instead he pulled her panties down to just above her knees and ran one teasing finger over her slit. She blushed, knowing how wet he was finding her entrance.

'OK,' he said. 'I accept the terms of your offer.'

Without another word, he pulled off her bra and panties, her blouse too, until all she wore were the high heels. Her cheeks flooded with heat. Luke was backing her up toward the wall of tyres with that naughty smile, and all she could think about were feeling his hands on her again. A small voice in her head reminded her that he hadn't actually fixed her tyre yet, that he could have sex with her right now and leave her still stranded, but as he fondled her breasts again, his fingers tweaking her nipples were so exciting that she couldn't bring herself to stop him.

Suddenly he stepped back. 'I guess you want that tyre fixed.'

'Right …'

'Shouldn't take long. But you have to give me something to look at while I work.'

Huh? She frowned, not understanding as he positioned her against the ladder. He lifted up her arms, leaning against her, and the weight of him felt so good on her body that it took a moment to notice he was tying her wrists to a ladder rung over her head.

'Hey!' she protested. 'You didn't say anything about tying me up!'

He laughed. 'Gotta make sure you don't welch, right? I fix that tyre, you could hop in the car and drive out without keeping up your end of the bargain.'

'I'm not going to welch!' The truth was that she was so turned on she was incapable of driving out of here without some kind of sexual release. 'Not to mention I'm kind of at your mercy.'

'Oh, come on now,' he said. 'I may be an opportunist, but I'm still a gentleman.'

The colour in her face deepened. Having her arms tied over her head forced her to arch her back and thrust out her breasts as if inviting Luke to play with them. Instead he stepped back, regarded her critically, then nodded with satisfaction. 'One last thing …'

He took out his phone. Realising he intended to snap her picture, she quickly shook her long hair across her face just before the phone camera clicked. Enraged, she jerked against her bonds, regretting the way it made her breasts bounce. 'Hey! You are not putting that online!'

'Relax. It's just a memento. You can't even see your face in it anyhow.'

He set the phone down and began to jack up the car as if it were just another job. She struggled to stay composed. No one had ever put her on display like this – naked in high heels with her arms tied over her head. Anyone who drove up to the garage right now would get an eyeful. Which was imminently possible even at this late hour, since any passing cars would see the lights on.

Keep it cool, Nadia, she told herself. She attempted to focus her thoughts by watching Luke. He was fitting on the new tyre like the pro he was, hard forearms flexed as he tightened the nuts. She couldn't help noting the whole thing was taking less than five minutes – hardly the infringement on his night as he'd insinuated. For this I'm prostituting myself out, she thought, then blushed. That was a harsh term for letting someone as sexy as Luke undress her and have his way with her. Barter was perhaps more appropriate.

And she couldn't deny that watching him work was nearly as arousing as him toying with her clit. He seemed so confident, so impudently sexy, so easy in his skin compared to the stuffy corporate executives she worked with. She closed her eyes, refusing to show how eager she was for her imminent ravishing. The garage's air-conditioning sent cool streams of air over her flushed and sensitive folds, making her desperate for stimulation. Her nipples longed to be sucked. What if – perish the thought – Luke decided that he actually *was* a gentleman and sent her off without any sex at all?

'All done.' He dropped the bolt, which fell to the floor with a clank, then headed over to the sink to wash up.

Nadia shifted restlessly against her bonds, the ladder pressing into the soft swell of her bottom. Half of her wanted Luke to untie her so she could run her hands all over

7

his hard young body and part of her wanted him to take her just like this, helpless and bound.

He walked up to her with a frown, studying her body as if she was a painting on the wall he'd mounted. Lightly he slapped her breasts, watching them bounce, then ran light fingertips over her nipples, still achingly hard.

'Please,' she begged finally.

His brows lifted. 'Please? I hope you mean you're going to please me. Because that was the term of our agreement.'

She nodded meekly.

He roughly unzipped his jeans, eyes hot with urgency. The game was over; Luke had fixed her tyre and now he was intent on using her body however he pleased and making her pay in full. She was breathless with anticipation of his cock pushing into her.

Instead he jumped onto the ladder, climbing the first few rungs with a foot on each side of her. What was he doing? She couldn't take her eyes from his thick, swollen cock, coming closer to her face with every rung.

He stopped, his silky erection in front of her mouth, and she understood exactly what he wanted.

Nadia took a deep breath. So he was serious about her pleasing him. OK, she could do this as long as it wasn't the only thing on the menu. Obediently she opened her lips. Luke pushed his swollen crown into her mouth. A salty-sweet drop of precome laced her tongue. So Luke was just as excited as she was, despite his insouciant attitude. With a surge of confidence, Nadia closed her lips over him, licking his head and teasing his most sensitive skin. He groaned, withdrawing slightly before pushing his shaft further into her mouth.

Nadia knew what to do. She turned her lips and tongue into a tight, wet tunnel as he began to thrust in and out of her mouth. From his rapid breathing, she could tell he was close to coming. Please touch me, she thought. Normally she liked to play with her clit when she gave a man head, but with her hands tied to the ladder, she was helpless to satisfy herself. It stoked the fire in her ever higher, her pussy aching to be fucked, as Luke enjoyed her mouth. He wouldn't really come like this, would he? Surely if he was a gentleman as he claimed, he would be sensitive enough to satisfy her –

His warm, salty come washed into her mouth. He had really done it, he had used her mouth to pay for the tyre without one thought for her own needs. That bastard.

He sighed deeply and stroked her auburn hair. '*Damn, that was good.*' He jumped to the floor and untied her hands.

Nadia leant back against the tyres, rubbing her wrists. Her inner thighs were still wet with excitement and her breasts were so filled with heat that she was of a mind to put his hands on her and beg him for release. But of course, that hadn't been part of the agreement. Damn him. Fighting for control, she began to pick up her blouse, skirt, and underwear.

'Hold on a minute,' Luke said. 'Did I say you were paid up yet?'

She looked up in disbelief. He'd already come; what more did he want? But he was leaning against her car with that smug grin, utterly in control.

He opened the door to her back seat. 'Climb in,' he told her. 'Sit on the edge of the seat and open your legs and show me your pussy.'

Weakly she did as he commanded. This was even worse torture, spreading her legs for him and knowing no stiff cock was going to slide between them. Still Luke seemed to enjoy studying her wet, tingling lips.

'Play with yourself,' he said. 'You know you're dying to.'

True, she had been dying to a few minutes ago when her wrists were bound, but that had just been as an aperitif for the main course – his hard cock inside her. Now that Luke was watching, it seemed more of a performance for him. Face burning with embarrassment, she began to stroke her clit.

'Nice,' he said. 'But don't stop there.'

Nadia sighed, succumbing to the spell of her own fingers tickling her clit and the delicious naughtiness of being watched. She spread her legs wider, showing him everything she had as her fingertips disappeared into her pink slit and worked past her initial tightness to stroke the most sensitive flesh of her cunt. She was drowning in delirious sensations of ecstasy, moaning so deeply that she didn't notice Luke was hard again until she felt him suddenly on top of her, pushing her on to the backseat.

Without a word, he pinned her arms down and drove his cock deep inside her.

A raw cry of pleasure and greed escaped from Nadia's throat. Never had being entered felt so intense, so feverish, her blood going incandescent as he worked every inch into her pulsing core. Luke held her down against the upholstery with primal ferocity, hips working agilely as he pounded her higher and higher into giddy, thrilling ecstasy. He knew exactly how to use his cock inside her, pushing against every sensitive inch of her. This was the naughty backseat sex she'd always craved but never dared to have. Her high heels fell from her feet as he fucked her, her breasts bouncing wildly with every thrust.

Luke grunted. 'Turn over.'

She was too dizzy to understand at first. 'What?'

He pulled out of her, making her protest with disappointment. Roughly but efficiently, he rolled her on to all fours. Taking her hips in his hands, he positioned his cock directly against her tingling slit. Then he waited.

Nadia wiggled her hips impatiently. Luke only stroked his swollen crown up and down her wet folds.

'Please,' she begged. She felt as if she would die if he didn't push back inside her. 'Please, Luke.'

'Please what?'

Despite being naked on all fours in her backseat, despite

knowing he had already seen and penetrated every inch of her pussy, her face burned at saying the words. 'Fuck me. Please. I can't stand it.'

His cock drove deep inside her, the cool, silky skin of his balls slapping against her inflamed flesh as he fucked her. Nadia groaned, rocking her hips back to meet his as he leant forward and cupped her tits. They were really fucking now, wild and hot and wet, her breasts jiggling against his palms. It had been years, maybe for ever, since a man had possessed her with this kind of unbridled, passionate mastery.

'Don't stop,' she cried hoarsely. 'Oh God.'

As Luke speared in and out of her, her long auburn hair hung in her face, clinging to her damp cheeks. A pulsing whirlpool of bliss was growing between her thighs and she couldn't speak as her nipples filled with heat. An intense shiver went through her body and then her orgasm burst like a hurricane in wet, euphoric throbs.

Luke groaned desperately and held her against him as his hips worked rapidly in the throes of his climax. Gradually she became aware that he was smiling down at her and stroking her hair.

Self-consciousness stole over her as he slid out of the backseat and helped her out. She felt more than a little embarrassed as she collected her clothes from the garage floor and began to dress. Her white silk blouse was dirty and there was a smudge of oil on her bra. Her legs were shaking almost too hard to step back into her heels. She pushed her hair back with a foolish smile and collected her purse.

Luke tossed her the car keys. 'There you go,' he said. 'Enjoy Lake Tahoe.'

'I will,' she said. 'Um, so about the tyre …'

'Free. You earned it.'

Nadia smiled and slid behind the wheel. As she began to back out, Luke leant in the window.

'One more thing,' he said. 'Your rear left tyre is looking

a little worn. If you want to replace it, you just stop in and see me on the way back Sunday.'

She grinned. 'I just might do that.'

She set off into the cool California night, lowering the windows to let the breeze in her hair. Putting her favourite CD on the car stereo, she couldn't stop smiling. Yes, she had learned her lesson. She would definitely be taking care of that left rear tyre.

Soul of Discretion
by Mary Borsellino

One of the reasons I'm in such high demand as a concierge is because of my excellent qualifications. I have an MBA, I'm licensed to drive every kind of vehicle in the standard hotel fleet, and I'm proficient in eight languages. I can hold numerous detailed schedules at the same time in my head, but always keep the computer's records up-to-date as well.

Basically, I'm the PA from heaven for an entire hotel's worth of people.

The other reason is that as well as having exemplary levels of competence, I'm extremely discreet. I wouldn't have been able to achieve one without the other: you think all that schooling pays for itself? While I'm certainly smart enough that I could've earned a scholarship without too much trouble, I've always preferred to make my own plans and do things on my own terms. So I became a call girl.

Not the kind you see in the tabloids and on the news from time to time, the beautiful, sculpted young things who've been caught in the bed of a political leader. No. I was the kind who was so good at what she did that no newspaper or TV crew ever got even an inkling that I was anywhere near the clients I worked for. Cultured, elegant, sexually acrobatic, and very, very good at staying out of sight.

I don't do that any more, because now that I'm a concierge I can make just as much money without nearly so much outlay on my reproductive health and personal grooming. I never have a hair out of place as a concierge, but I also don't have to spend hundreds of dollars a month keeping my hair strictly confined to my head. I figured at 28 it was probably time to have at least a little bit of pubic hair for a change.

And it isn't as if I've left the life behind entirely. I still have just as many high-end maître ds and shady cocaine suppliers in my speed-dial as I ever did, only now I call them on behalf of hotel guests instead of clients, and my cut of the take is higher.

I still have a lot of the same friends that I met in that old life as well, so from time to time my phone rings quietly in the pocket of my impeccable grey suit jacket, and I hear a variation of the call I received last week. Of course, matters don't always turn out as they did on that occasion.

'Cara, you absolutely cannot pass this up, I swear to God.'

'Mm-hm?' I asked noncommittally. I hadn't spoken to Mitchell in a while, but I'd been turning down "once in a lifetime chances" ever since the day I quit the business. I couldn't imagine anything that'd be different about this one.

'An old buddy of mine is tour managing for Liam Lucifer and he needs a girl at the hotel tonight. He doesn't want to ask the guest services desk there – too many bad experiences with people selling stories to the tabloids, you know how it is. So my buddy gets Liam to call me, because my buddy knows I can find a girl who's good to keep her mouth shut. Nobody's better at that than you, Cara. You're cream of the crop.'

'I'm not even part of the "crop" any more, Mitch,' I retorted. 'And Liam Lucifer's the biggest rock star in the world right now. I'm sure he can get a hundred girls just as hot as me from the groupie pool for nothing.'

'No can do. They'd blog the whole thing before they'd left the room. Liam values his privacy pretty highly. Highly enough to pay top dollar.'

I want to make it absolutely clear before I go any further

that I've never let my work life overlap with my home life. The second that happens is the second things start to get messy.

Not complicated; I can handle complicated just fine. That's practically in my job description. Messy, though, I don't like. So it's always been my policy to avoid clients I have any kind of emotion about. If I've slept with a candidate, I don't vote in the election. Things like that.

Liam Lucifer's album had been in my car stereo ever since it came out. I knew the words to every song within the first week. The photo of Liam on the CD cover showed him with his lip curled in a sneer and a streak of red greasepaint down over his forehead and one eye, like a punk rock David Bowie. I wanted to knot my fingers in the thick, black curls of his hair and bite at the lush fullness of his lip.

When I'd been an escort, those thoughts alone would have been more than enough reason for me to turn down Mitchell's offer. But I wasn't an escort any more, and there was nothing to stop me from dabbling in a little illicit fun with my favourite rock star, and making a mint while I was at it.

'OK. But you owe me one, Mitch.'

I still have some of my old clothes, but quickly decided not to wear any of them. My work as a concierge has necessitated more than enough evening wear and high heels, and it seemed sensible for my mental health not to mix up my former life with my current one. Even if I was getting dressed up to go have a lot of sex in exchange for a lot of money.

I caught a cab to the hotel Mitchell had given me the name of, and nodded hello to the concierge at work behind his counter in the lobby. Privately I agreed with Mitchell's assessment of him – he didn't look like someone who'd be able to resist sweet-talk from a tabloid writer.

Liam answered his own door, and was alone in his suite. His dark hair was damp from the shower, his rock-star make-up scrubbed from his unexpectedly freckled face. His T-shirt and jeans looked broken-in and comfortable, and not much like the clothes I was used to seeing on jobs like this.

Of course, I'd never had a job quite like this one before, really.

'Hey! Cara, right?' he said, beckoning me inside and closing the door. 'There's all kinds of drinks in the minibar if you want any, and I've got some weed in my luggage somewhere if you want that.'

I decided it would be a good idea to use the same policy I'd had when I was a call girl: no intoxicants on the job. I smiled and shook my head.

'Is a cheque OK? I can get cash out but you'll have to give me a minute to go down to the ATM.'

I noticed that his feet were bare, toenails painted a dark iridescent blue. A small reminder that the affable, attractive man in front of me was a bona fide rock-and-roll superstar.

'A cheque's fine,' I assured him, reaching one of my hands behind me to catch the top of the zipper on the low backline of my dress, parting the teeth slowly so the thin shoulder straps would slip down in one graceful motion.

'I've left the amount blank. Mitchell told me that's what you prefer. So you can add up all the things we do after we're done and just write in the total yourself.'

'It's simpler that way,' I explained, taking the offered check and slipping it into my oversized beaded purse, which was otherwise full of condoms, lubricants, and a few of my favourite sex toys. I noticed Liam's eyes light up at the sight of the light leather flogger.

A teasing smirk played at his full lips. 'But what if there's something I want and I need to check if I can afford it before we do it?'

I smirked right back, letting my dress slide down my body and pool, discarded, around my ankles and feet. 'If you need to check, you can't afford it.'

Liam gave me a long, appreciative look, taking in my

suspender stockings and silk panties, the half-cup bra which left my hard pink nipples exposed above the thin edge of lace.

'First course is definitely oral,' he declared, pulling his T-shirt up over his head. No tattoos, another scatter of those surprising freckles, one nipple pierced with a simple steel barbell. Good muscle tone.

'Sure,' I said, going to my bag and pulling out one of the flavoured condoms. Liam put his hand on my arm, stopping me as I moved to tear the wrapper open.

'Rubbers are non-negoti–' I started to say before Liam shook his head, cutting me off.

'Oh, no, no, of course. I just meant … I want to go down on you. Is that allowed?'

I gave a pointed glance down at his body. He'd removed his jeans and was completely naked now, and his impressive cock was very visibly interested in the circumstances. My heart rate picked up a little at the thought of that thick, warm flesh in my mouth, and I had to remind myself sternly that that wasn't what he wanted. Oh well, maybe later.

I replaced the condom in my bag and drew out a dental dam instead, handing it to Liam and then bending to remove my stockings and panties before moving towards the lushly decorated king-sized bed.

'You've got pubic hair, thank God,' Liam noted appreciatively, kneeling at the end of the bed and parting my bare legs where I sat at the edge. 'I didn't expect that, but I hoped. I hate playing when there's no grass on the field, you know?'

'I know that's a terrible phrase nobody should utter,' I told him, helping him put the dam in place.

Liam was serious about the task before him from the moment he lowered his head. I've had my share of cunnilingus, both giving and receiving, and it was clear to me that Liam Lucifer is one of those people who truly loves eating out a woman.

He used his fingers, lips, teeth, tongue, nose; nuzzling up and down my inner lips as they plumped with heat and parted, moist and slick under their thin latex sheet. He teased my clit with the very tips of his fingers, light enough and slow enough that after a while of this attention my thighs began to shake and my hips began to buck, aching for more and firmer contact.

'Fuck, fuck, harder, yes,' I groaned out through clenched teeth, arching my back. I could feel my orgasm, fluttering like a huge winged creature, just beyond my grasp. 'Fuck, your mouth is so fucking good.'

Liam lapped and sucked at me with an urgency of his own now, one of his hands wrapped around his cock and stroking at a rapid, sloppy pace. He was moaning against me, the vibrations pulsing through every one of my nerve-endings and dragging my climax out of me with a choked cry. Liam followed with a peak of his own just a few seconds later, panting hotly against my thigh, mouth slack with desire and well used with pressure against my flesh.

He grinned up at me, a happy, well-fucked rock star. 'Satisfactory beginning?' he asked.

I nodded, motioning for him to clean himself off and join me on the bed. 'What else would you like to do, once we've caught our breath?'

He grabbed a bottle of water from the minibar, taking a few big swallows, sweat gleaming on his throat as he tipped his head back.

'You do pegging? he checked. I nodded again. 'Then pegging, thanks. Maybe a handjob or a blowjob just beforehand, to get me relaxed. A little flogging after, when I'm high enough on sex to want the pain. Your tits are fucking amazing, so I might fuck them later if I have any spunk left in me by then.' He laughed lightly. 'And some good old missionary with you on top to finish. How's that sound?'

'An excellent selection. I like a man who knows what he

wants.'

'And I like a woman who can provide it,' Liam countered. 'Mitchell wasn't sure if he'd be able to get you. I'm very glad he did.'

'I wasn't certain at first,' I confessed. 'I don't do this all that often any more. You're an exception.'

'What made you decide to agree?'

I gave him my most mysterious smile. 'I'm sure Mitchell told you that my best talent is for keeping secrets, Mr Lucifer. Some things, a lady never tells.'

Filthy White Dress
by Fulani

Chloe sits in the Aztec Bar, sipping a mocha coffee. The bar is nowhere near Mexico – it's on the third floor of a city centre hotel – and the name was probably chosen to reflect the gaudy décor in maroon and gold.

The men in suits who populate this bar, most of them networking, negotiating, buying or selling, look in Chloe's direction occasionally. Their eyes register curiosity or, sometimes, lust. She knows what they're thinking. They're trying to work out if she's someone's mistress or lover, a professional escort waiting for a client, or a prostitute. They're thinking this because she's half their age, has out-of-the-bottle chestnut hair almost long enough to sit on, and wears a little black dress that shows a lot of leg and ankle boots with four-inch heels.

The fact is, she's reading a book called *Drama/Theatre/Performance* and getting her head around the theories of action, alienation, catharsis, character, and representation. She's reading it on her Kindle, though, so for all anyone else in the room knows she could be reading some hot erotica.

She's reading the book because she's waiting for someone to come down from the fifth floor.

It's the more attractive of the men on the fifth floor, the one in the vintage pea jacket and open-necked dress shirt, who appears through the elevator doors. He was introduced to her as Dr Vogel. Vogel, meaning "bird" in Dutch, an appropriate name for someone with almost luminous eyes and a sharp nose. He's maybe in his early thirties, looks fit, and in other circumstances she might fancy him.

'I'm afraid they offered the spot elsewhere,' he says. 'You were a strong contender, but the marketing people -'

'– wanted someone else they thought would better represent the qualities of the product?' Chloe finishes the sentence for him. It's not like she hasn't been there before. Years in drama school, dozens of stage shows and a couple of minor film parts, and she's still in the rat-race to get 15 seconds of fame in a commercial for a new chocolate bar.

At least she'd made the shortlist this time. Making the shortlist, though, doesn't pay the rent.

She'd sucked it, licked it, rubbed it across her face, done everything they'd demanded to bring out its character and induce viewers to desire the chocolate.

Chloe sighs and shrugs, aware that half the men in the bar are now trying to work out if Dr Vogel is a client, lover, or sugar daddy. The idea of a "confectionary psychologist", which is how he'd been described, being a "sugar daddy" sends a playful if sardonic twist to the corner of her mouth.

'It's slightly unprofessional,' the good doctor is saying, 'but I wondered if dinner on Friday might be possible for you? It might be a slight compensation for the … other thing.'

Well, why not? She doesn't exactly need to clear her schedule.

'By the way, if you could wear something white, I'd be particularly grateful.'

She's had more bizarre suggestions in the past.

The starters cost more than Chloe's weekly supermarket shopping. A glass of wine costs more than the white bodycon dress she'd bought from eBay.

Oh well. She's an actress, isn't she? She knows how to act rich. She enjoys the pigeon breast medallions in plum sauce. Goes with the flow of wine; white with the starter, red with the main course, a sweet dessert wine to follow. Vogel, who never actually tells her his first name, is a sparkling conversationalist.

She feels like a pro escort. Gets into the character a bit.

Is she going to let him take her home and fuck her? Now she's in character, she's going to be the one leading him to bed. Or the living room carpet, the back of his car, or wherever he wants.

In the darkness of the side street where he's parked his car, Chloe runs her hand down the front of his shirt, allowing her fingers to rest on his belt buckle. She's completely up for unfastening the buckle and giving him a blowjob there and then.

He smiles at her, a perverted, filthy smile.

'Actually I wasn't going to ask you for sex …'

She arches an eyebrow. He's the first man, ever, to say that to her.

'The thing about fetishes,' he says, 'is that they don't just mean sex with a twist. They mean the twist takes over from the sex completely. The kink itself becomes the sex.'

Momentary images in Chloe's head: Dr Vogel in leather, or rubber, or stockings. Dr Vogel spanking her, being spanked by her, Dr Vogel tying her to the bed before fucking her, or telling her that he has a wife and wants to take Chloe home for a threesome.

She's not an innocent. You don't hang out in drama school, with everyone around you exploring their psyche and having cathartic moments, and not get just a little bit liberated, a little bit corrupted. So none of these things are off-limits, none are turn-offs.

And then he asks her to rub herself against the brick wall of the building. Hmm …

She'd had to hold back at the casting interview, with that bar of chocolate. Now she's completely uninhibited. Works that wall like a pole dancer works a pole. Slides her arse along the rough, grimy surface like she's hoping the bricks will melt under her pressure, flow and distend until there's a masonry cock trying to penetrate her. She slides her hips seductively, feeling the irregularities, the exposed corners where mortar's worn away. They chew at the thin material of the dress, leaving tiny ragged tears. Arches her back and turns, squeezing her breasts against the wall, dragging them up and down its cool firmness until it feels like she might wear it away, until friction makes her nipples hard.

Chloe turns back to the doctor, half-expecting to see him with his cock standing proudly exposed. He certainly has an erection, but it's still in his pants. She looks down at the dress, disfigured by filthy black streaks and ripped in places, exposing her skin on the belly, buttocks, and thighs.

'Thank you.' His voice is thick, choked with emotion that seems to come from far away and long ago. His childhood, perhaps?

'And now?' She rubs up against him, playfully, expecting cock in her mouth or pussy.

He smiles wanly. 'It's a rule of mine. No sex on the first date.'

Gentlemanly, he drives her home. Outside, he kisses her chastely and makes one last request.

'Please – take the dress off and give it to me.'

'Only if you tell me what you're going to do with it,'

He coughs. Is he embarrassed?

'Since you ask, I shall take it home, take it to bed with me, and probably masturbate into it. How does that make you feel?'

Chloe frowns. 'It's not exactly what I expected from the evening. But then people are … unpredictable. They have different tastes, don't they?'

She climbs out of the car, strips to her underwear, hands him the soiled garment and is astonished when he hands her a roll of banknotes.

'Can we do this again? Same time next week?'

She walks the twenty yards to her front door, wearing bra, G-string, and heels, a clutch purse in one hand and hard currency in the other, feeling a sudden sense of lightness and liberation. Goes to bed with a vibrator, thinking about what Dr Vogel is doing with her dress. Goes to sleep with questions circling in her head that she can't quite put into words.

Friday comes around. Chloe has a white tube dress, clingy from bust to hips and with a long side split that shows the entire length of her leg. Chooses steak in the restaurant, artfully allows some of the juices to dribble down her chin, making sure he sees it before she uses her napkin. Afterwards he drives them to the Heath, a green lung in the city that's used, this time of night, by couples both straight and gay who like sex outdoors, along with prostitutes and the occasional voyeur. He watches as she makes love to a tree, savouring the gnarled texture of the bark. She can understand why some people hug trees. He watches as she rolls, laughing and libidinous, on the grass. She's been reading stuff on the Internet: there used to be an all-female band called Rockbitch that grew out of a pagan collective. The women sometimes did a ceremony they called "fucking the ground". On the Heath, looking out over city lights in the distance, it certainly feels like there's some energy exchange going on.

The doctor looks on, hypnotised by her performance. He's not so much a sharp-eyed bird of prey as a deer transfixed in the spotlight of her exotic, erotic gyrations.

The ground pulls and rubs at her dress, leaving her bare-breasted. When she finally stands, the garment stays on her only because it's bunched around her hips. She steps out of it gracefully, revealing the fact that she'd worn nothing under it. He doesn't react and she knows he wouldn't, because his idea of sexual exhibitionism is not the same as hers. Chloe's naked for her, not him. She gathers up the dirty fabric in one hand, slowly and purposefully moves to him, unfastens his belt, reveals his engorged cock. She drapes the dress hem over the cock, allowing the material to drag across it, then squeezes gently.

'Trust me,' she whispers in his ear. And he comes, shoots hot spunk captured by the inner folds of the soft, soiled material.

He takes her home, riding naked in his car, hands her a wad of notes even larger than before.

Friday comes around. Chloe has a white halter-neck dress, figure-hugging with a ruched hem that comes just above the knee. Has the swordfish steak with a lambs' kidney sauce. They've talked and texted during the week. Dr Vogel is at least frank about his sex life. Every week he sees a woman in black – a pro domme; a woman in red – a prostitute, and Chloe. He sees white as a representation of innocence, freshness, clarity, catharsis.

Then he drives her out to an old industrial district, a closed-down and burned-out factory. She does the dirty along a rusted chain-link fence, the remains of an oil tank, the sooty, twisted and burned ironwork.

She gets off on it; the idea of filth as erotic. Because, after all, porn is sometimes called "filthy" and "dirty"; Chloe's begun to relate to the idea that firth and dirt can be pornographic …

She presses her pelvis against Dr Vogel's groin. Feels the massive, iron-hard crection there.

'I think,' she says provocatively, 'you should just rip the dress off my body.' She's looking into his eyes, but they're focused on the inside of his head and not on her. His fingers grip the material between her breasts; the sensation shocks her because it's the first time he's touched her skin. Then he's clawing at her, tearing the material, strong hands warm and frantic against her body. He pushes her and then yanks fiercely at the dress; Chloe loses her balance, bouncing off the links of the fence. The sudden violence of his move, its dissonance from his usual civilised behaviour, is weirdly thrilling. Feels like she's broken through a barrier. As he pulls the dress off her in shreds, Chloe's overcome with an urgent need. Takes the doctor's free hand, crams the knuckles hard against her pussy, grinds against them.

Says corny stuff like, 'Yes yes do it to me yes I'm coming I'm I'm ...' and then the low animal moan of the orgasm itself chainsawing its way through her body. And the doctor's grunting, hips jerking involuntarily.

'That,' he says when he's recovered himself, 'hasn't happened to me since puberty.'

'What hasn't?'

But she knows. She can smell the hot, sticky fluid. He's come in his underwear.

It occurs to her she still doesn't know what kind of underwear he favours. Boxers, tighty whities, thong, leather posing pouch with studs on the inside ...?

When he drops her at home, being naked on the street at two in the morning feels strangely normal. And there's a roll of banknotes in her hand, the transaction as routine and as slutty as a prostitute's fee. Though don't prostitutes ask for the cash upfront? And not many would get *this* high a fee.

The money, actually, is something Chloe thinks about a lot. It may be small change to Dr Vogel but, until recently, she's been a student on a tight budget and now she's trying to be a working actress with no steady income. In the space of three weeks she's earned what she regards as around three months' income, less the cost of three white dresses at bargain eBay prices.

Sex is something she thinks about as well. He doesn't fuck her. She could have a boyfriend, a lover, a series of one-night stands. She gets hit on often enough. If she walked from home to the corner store she could easily come back with bread, milk, and a guy with a dazed grin and his dick bursting out of his jeans. But that's not what she wants. She wants someone who'll act exactly like she tells them to. Someone like …

… a male escort. Who, it turns out, isn't at all expensive compared with the money Dr Vogel has been giving her.

Her stunt dick – which is how she thinks of him – is Olivier. That's probably not his real name, but names aren't important. She meets him in the place where it all started, the Aztec Bar. She's chosen him because he has shoulder-length hair and looks, in her mind at least, like a singer in a rock band. Turns out he's the bass player, but the band hasn't even had its first gig yet. He's dressed entirely in black, like she instructed, and it complements her dress. She's chosen a white dress that's artfully constructed out of holes and slits.

Olivier is somewhat up himself but nonetheless personable. He tells her about the band, about his bass guitar, and about how the fingerwork on a fretless guitar neck is a skill that can be transferred into all kinds of situations. He shows her the span of his fingers and the fact he's not wearing rings. His fingernails are trimmed and clean. Clit-friendly.

He seems relieved that she's not middle-aged, and not a capricious and dominating female exec. 'They've sent me to quite a few of those,' he says openly. 'I think the agency figures they're a baptism of fire, if I could deal with those situations they'd give me a better class of client.' Sounds like a backhanded compliment.

She tells Olivier she'd like to go for a walk with him. And it's only on the way out she realises that, all this time, Dr Vogel has been sitting on the other side of the bar – with a blonde woman in a red button-through summer dress that's a couple of sizes too small for her. The red of the dress looks mismatched against the maroon walls of the bar and the blonde doesn't quite match the gold trim that picks out the woodwork.

Judging by the way she's looking, his eyes have been on Chloe for the last half-hour. Or maybe on the skin showing through the slits and holes. That's the thing about dresses: he's seen her naked and yet just a sliver of skin, artfully framed with material, can be more attention-grabbing.

'Where are we going?' Olivier asks.

'Well …' Why not tell him? 'I thought I'd take you down to the canal, the area just beyond the big dance clubs, where there's some derelict land. We can find somewhere private, like all the young couples who go down there from the clubs, and you can fuck me stupid. Are you OK with that?'

She wonders for a moment if he's going to say sex isn't part of the service, or costs extra. Instead he just grins.

'Sounds good to me …'

So good he can't keep his hands, with their long finger-span, to himself. Not that Chloe wants him to. They find the holes and slits in her dress, feel warm against bare skin. And discover that the dress, which looks like any underwear would need to be specially designed not to show, isn't hiding any underwear.

Ten minutes later she's propped against an old concrete post, canted at a 45-degree angle. Her dress is around her waist, her legs spread, his tongue between them. Olivier's worth the money: feels like he could tie a knot in her clit with that tongue. And his fingers are playing the tendons in her thighs like they're thick, juicy bass strings.

'Condom in my purse,' she pants.

'Condom in my pocket,' he replies. But his lips are still crushed against her labia, so him just saying the words sends a thrill through her body and right the way up to her skull.

He flips her over, taking her from behind. Each thrust lifts her on her spread heels. Pushes in far enough, it's way past the G-spot, the tip of his cock massaging her anterior fornix. If it goes any further it will surely bruise her lungs.

Muscle spasms in her thighs mean her legs won't support her, he's taking the whole of her weight on his cock. She's literally impaled on it. She can't move. As if she'd want to … And her breasts are rubbing against the rough concrete edges of the post, the exact same erotic sensations she's had with the doctor.

Her climax is normally a ripple that turns into a wave and then a flood. This time it's more like a furious deluge that just sweeps her away under its brutal impact.

'You know what?' Olivier asks.

She doesn't know what. She's slumped against the post, still dazed, her breasts rubbed raw against the concrete and pussy feeling heavily abused. She looks at him with half-closed eyes.

'Towards the end, there, another couple were in the shadows, maybe twenty yards away, and I think they were screwing too. Believe it or not, I've never had that before. That sense of doing it in public, being watched. It was a real turn-on. I may have to become an exhibitionist.'

She laughs. 'You use your fingers like that in public already, you were already an exhibitionist!'

Under the street lights, he looks at her, concerned. 'Your dress is filthy!'

She shrugs, smiles. 'Just the way I like it!'

Dr Vogel seems to have influenced her a little more than she might have expected.

She leaves Olivier by the entrance to the Aztec Bar. The sex was brilliant but she needs to be alone with her feelings about it.

The following morning there's an email.

I hope you don't mind, but having seen you in the bar we followed you and your partner. Watched you. It was beautiful, and my companion in red was finally able to make me come.

Well, there's a confession. He has the woman for sex, but can only come while thinking about besmirched innocence. That's his catharsis.

There's more.

Can I buy that dress from you?

Friday. They have dinner as usual, or at least it now feels like it's usual. She hands him the dress right there in the restaurant and is gratified by his startled excitement.

'He's not my partner,' she says casually. How much should she tell him? 'He's just ... someone I met.'

'I shall have to pay you double,' he says. And then he has a proposal. He's beginning to feel more ... integrated. Less alienated. Would she be interested, he wants to know, in meeting him in other colours. Red, for example, or black?

Chloe knows the implications of the colours, what each would involve in terms of activities. And that's OK because she does actually fancy the guy despite his kink. Maybe even because of it, now. The idea of colour-coded sex is intriguing.

She doesn't say that, though.

'How would you feel,' she asks, 'about patterns? I saw this Sixties-style dress the other day. Red, white, and black stripes.'

And can't stop herself chuckling when his suddenly vacant expression tells her he's literally come in his pants.

The Best Handjob in the North
by Victoria Blisse

I work in one of those car wash places, the type where they do it all by hand. It has a huge yellow sign that proclaims in loud, red lettering that this is THE BEST HANDJOB IN THE NORTH. I hate it. I get wet and my white T-shirt clings to my ample bosom. I swear the lads splash me on purpose most times. I get so very cold - I work in Manchester, not the flipping Bahamas - and I'm paid a pittance, but what else is there for someone uninterested in study and with only a minimum number of qualifications?

One good thing about it is I get decent tips, especially on those days when I am soaked to the skin and my top clings to all my curves. If I bat my eyelashes and smile seductively I am always guaranteed a substantial bonus for my troubles. I think the guys are jealous of me; that's probably why they don't talk to me much.

'Bloody freezing,' I groan one dark, dank November morning, 'I'm going to have to give this up and get a real job soon.'

No one answers me as I'm the only person in at 8 a.m. on a Monday but I've got to keep myself amused somehow. I sit on a plastic garden chair. It was white once, I'm sure, but these days it's more a Mancunian morning grey. I pull my hat down over my ears and settle in. No one wants their cars washed on a Monday morning but the boss hates to think he might miss even one tiny bit of trade. His middle name is Ebenezer - or at least it should be.

So I'm rather surprised when a big, sleek, black car pulls in a few moments later. Ironically I'm not very good at identifying cars but this one has "money" written all over it. So does the guy who winds down the window. He is wearing a charcoal suit, the shirt beneath it bright white, the same colour as his teeth. His black hair sweeps over his forehead in a curve that indicates it has more to do with good grooming and time stood in front of a mirror than genes.

'So, is the sign true, then?' he asks with an arched brow and a wicked smirk.

'Very true.' I flash him a smirk of my own, knowing that a little sexual innuendo won't harm my chances of a good tip.

'Then show me.'

'Certainly, sir. Would you like the regular or the deluxe treatment?'

'I want the best handjob in the north, love, and I want it from you.'

'Oh, you can't afford me,' I quip, his intense stare burning into my skin and starting a fever inside me.

'What do you charge?'

'For the best?'

'Yes, the best. Your fingers clenched around my dick.'

I meet his gaze. My cheeks burn like embers but I'm not going to let him win so easily.

'I told you, you can't afford it.'

'How much?' he insists. I pluck a ridiculous figure from the air.

'A grand.'

'OK,' he replies, not one hair on his well-coiffured head ruffled.

'Up front and in cash,' I add.

'Sure.' He looks away for the first time and withdraws crisp £50 notes from his wallet. I've never seen a £50 note before, let alone multiples of them.

'There, one thousand.'

'Right, well, erm, yes.'

'Count it by all means,' he says.

I don't know how to respond. I mean, I know how I should respond. This guy is offering to buy my sexual services. I should be ringing 999 and summoning the police to take away the disgusting pervert. But I have more money in my hand than I'd ever held before. It would pay for so much, and what would I have to do for it? Next to nothing.

'I must clean your car first.' I strip off my navy blue fleece.

'Sure,' he replies, 'I might as well get my money's worth.'

I'm not sure why I tell him that, but I think I can gather my thoughts and my courage while I wash. I do it all on automatic pilot. I start at the back and move round to the front wiping suds on with my big, yellow sponge. At the hood I lean over more to emphasise my boobs and my arse and I'm rewarded by seeing him paying great attention to both areas.

Washing off the suds is the worst bit. The cold water from the hose is like ice so late in the year. I do splash myself a little more than is strictly necessary, though. The iciness perks up my nipples so nicely and I don't think the cocky stranger will mind. I'm struck by just how much of a slut I am being. I'm going to wank off some man and I don't even know his name.

'I think it's squeaky clean now, love, and my dick is aching. Jump in.' He gestures with his head to the seat beside him. I nod and slowly drop my cloth. I walk round slowly and open the door.

'Ah, no, no, no. I can't have you getting in here with that wet T-shirt on, you'll ruin my seats. Take it off.'

'What?' I snap.

His stern look makes me realise he is paying a lot of money for my services and, as the boss says, the customer is always right.

I reluctantly hook my fingers under my top and pull it off. I drop it to the ground then dive into the car, slamming the door behind me.

'That's better,' he smiles, 'much better. Now get to it.'

He stretches back against the black leather seat and pushes his crotch up lewdly. I can see the outline of his erection quite clearly and I lick my lips nervously. If I'm totally honest with myself, I am very excited. My nipples are not just responding to the cold and if I slipped my hand beneath the stretchy waistband of my jogging bottoms and down between my thighs I would coat my fingers liberally with my juices.

I'm not allowed to do that, though; it's what's in his pants that I need to concentrate on. I take a deep breath and reach out towards him.

'That's it,' he whispers as he watches my delicate fingers fiddle with his button-down pants. I can feel the quality in the material as each button slips through with a crisp clunk. I'm slightly shocked when I press my fingers into the opening and find hot, hard man not soft cotton underwear. I wonder if he's planned this in advance. I'm not sure if that excites or scares me but the cock that unfurls as I ease it from under the expensive trousers definitely excites me.

I stroke my fingers up and down it for a moment, trailing around the bulbous tip and around the thick shaft, tickling down into the sparse, dark hair that covers his large, warm balls. I'm rewarded by a catch in his breathing and an extended expiration of air that tickles across my cheek as I lean close to him. I position my hand around his shaft, noting how it fits so nicely there.

I glance towards him and his steely gaze. He's watching my every move intently. I suppose I would too if I'd paid someone an obscene amount of money to wank me off. I've become so engrossed with his cock that I've forgotten I'm sitting in a car, in my place of work, with my top off and the boss and boys due to arrive at - well, any moment. I look around nervously but everything is still quiet so I decide to get back to the task in hand. I do not want my boss to discover me like this, though the thought of it sends a shock of pleasure through my body.

I squeeze my fingers around his stiff erection and move my hand up and then down in one slow stroke. I keep doing this over and over building speed and pressure until I hear the word "Yes!" hiss from between his lips, just beside my ear. His breath caressing me is like a kiss; it feels so intimate being this close to a man I don't even know.

Something strikes me then. I want to please him. I want to give him the best damn handjob of his life and I want him to remember me and this moment for the rest of his existence. I know I will remember it, the day I whored myself for cash. I should burn with humiliation at that fact and I do, but I think I like it. I like the idea that some man is willing to pay for my services. I enjoy being in control, being the focus of his lust.

I reach my left hand over and slip it down to his balls. I'm leaning against his body now and he's slipped his arm around my shoulder. It feels incredibly intimate and I love the weight of his arm around me, the warmth of it and the strength in it. His fingers stroke down the flesh just below my shoulder to the rhythm of my wanking.

'That's it, love,' he gasps, his hips lifting and forcing his erection through my hand. I know he's not far from coming. 'Fuck, yes, that's it.'

I cup his balls as I continue to stroke his shaft which throbs beneath my fingers. The pulse is like a pump and moments later I watch as white, thick come arcs into the air and cascades down over my fingers. I continue to stroke, gently and firmly, as he grunts out his orgasm. The scent will be for ever etched in my memory. Woody leather, cheap soap suds, and potent, masculine ejaculation that reminds me of burnt-down bonfires.

I continue to lean against him for a moment, his shuddering breaths rocking his ribcage beside me. I slowly release his cock and lift my fingers to my lips. I engage eye contact and lick each digit clean. He tastes of the sea and fresh linen, like when I grip my pillowcase between my teeth to stop myself from screaming as I come.

'Thanks, love,' he says as I lick my lips. He pulls away from me and I sit back in my seat. 'Worth every penny.'

I smile and look around; no one has arrived yet but I can see a familiar car on the main road.

'Shit, the boss is here.' I open the door and pick up my T-shirt then clamber out to put it on.

'Hey -' he pulls my attention back to him before I slam the passenger door shut '- take this.'

He offers me a small rectangle of paper.

'And ring me. I'd be interested in purchasing more of your services.'

'I'm not a whore,' I gasp but I take the card as he insistently pushes it towards me.

'Oh, you are now, love, and a very good one at that.'

I slam the passenger door shut and, seconds later, his engine fires up and the car pulls away with a low purr that vibrates in my cunt. I just zip up my fleece after stuffing my ill-gotten gains into my bra before my boss walks across the forecourt to me.

'See, I told you it was worth opening so early, you've had a job already.'

And he's more correct than he can ever imagine.

I don't think I engage my brain once for the rest of the day. I'm too busy thinking about my pussy. I need relief and I can't get it, not at work. Even the toilet has paper-thin walls and the boss times your potty breaks. I know I wouldn't take long to come but I want to enjoy the experience so I save it all up until I got home.

I run up the stairs to my tiny flat, slam the door shut

behind me, strip off my fleece, and throw it to the ground. I kick off my trainers and thick socks then slip down my trousers and knickers. I walk over towards my bedroom and pull off my still damp T-shirt but I keep on my bra, the crispy notes warm and crinkly against my skin, a reminder of the lewd act I committed earlier in the day.

My bed is still as crinkled as when I left it, no time or inclination to make it before work. I dive on to the bed, springs creaking as I pull the duvet over my chilled skin. My fingers are cold and red and I attempt to warm them by stroking down my throat to my breasts, feeling their meaty warmth beneath the crinkly surface of all those notes, the payment for my sexual services.

I revel in being a whore as my hands slip lower and between my thighs, the tips slowly thawing as I plunge them between my sticky lips. I'm hot and damp down there, my clit is prominent, and the zings of pleasure explode through my body from the very first stroke of my excited nub.

I remember his cock, the paradoxical power of soft and hard as it slipped through my fingers and that scent, the smell of a seedy sex scene in public. I come hard, legs clamping around my hand, body curling, sound screaming from me and probably scaring the neighbour. I'm a slut - no, more so I'm a whore, I've been paid for my services. I don't feel ashamed, I feel proud of my curves, the curves so many people have poked fun at over the years. My abundant body is worth paying for.

I pull the money out from my bra, smooth down each note and add it up as I go. As I pull out another wodge his card falls out on the bed. One side is printed immaculately but on the back is scrawled a mobile number. I check the card; it reveals to me his name.

Richard. Well, it makes sense. He is a bit of a dick.

I put my money away and stare at the card. I know I should throw it away, take the money, and run. One paid-for handjob doesn't make me a prostitute and the influx of cash will pay for some new clothes, maybe a weekend trip to the seaside or a really wild night out with my mates. But I think about how much money I could make if I fucked him. I think about how it would feel to ride his cock, the satisfaction of his dirty money in my pocket and the pleasure of sex, sex with him.

I text him in the end, too scared to ring.

It was the greatest handjob, right? What do you want to try out next? Alison from the car wash x

The reply pings back within seconds.

I want to fuck you. How much for that?

I think for a moment.

Ten grand.

I wait impatiently until my phone chimes again.

Five grand and the best orgasm of your life.

My heart flutters, my breath catches in my throat and I feel light-headed.

Five up front but if you don't make me come I get the other five afterwards.

I'm amazed when he agrees. He tells me to meet him at a certain place, a place lovers know and go to when they want privacy but the thrill of the possibility of being caught. A country lane that ends in a field and nothing more. I berate myself as I climb into my reliable old rust bucket and head for the hills. I should not be doing this; it's against every piece of safety advice I've ever received, but I don't turn back.

He's there when I arrive. I'd recognise his car anywhere. I pull up next to him and switch off my engine. I unclick the safety belt and take a deep breath. I look to my left and he is there. He dips his head in greeting and smirks. Or maybe that is his usual look, the casual grin that is so wicked and so promising at the same time. I step out of the car and smooth the skirt down my legs. I'd dressed up carefully to show off my feminine assets. I wanted to show him exactly what I've got. My hair is down, and the brown curls bob on my shoulders as I walk carefully over to the passenger door of his car through the persistent drizzle of a northern winter's night.

'Hello again, love,' he says as I sit down on the seat beside him. The cold leather sticks to the back of my knees. 'You scrub up well.'

'Gee, thanks,' I reply with a snarl, my stomach joining in, but with a growl of arousal not reprisal.

'So I want to fuck you this time. I want to feel your cunt around my dick. Here's your money.'

He passes me a brown envelope. It seems so incredibly seedy. My heartbeat quickens.

'But you have to make me come or I get another five grand, right?'

'Sure,' he replies, 'but I am going to make you come, love, I'm going to make you scream.'

'We'll see about that,' I reply. 'Shall we take our business to the back seat?'

I hope my voice shows no hint of my nerves as he replies in the affirmative and exits his side of the car. I get out and he calls me over to his side. I walk over to him, noting his height, the width of his shoulders, the casual elegance of his jeans, and the warm black jacket on top, labelled no doubt but so expensive the label is small and fine and probably in gold lettering. He opens the back door and stands leaning against it, his hip cocked.

'Hitch up that skirt as you get in,' he says, 'I don't want it in my way.'

I obey his order and it reveals my lack of underwear.

'Oh, what a slut you are.' He growls as I sit down on the edge of the back seat. He follows me in, his frame filling the door frame and his hands pushing me back forcefully. He doesn't bother to close the door behind him - no one else is around on such a cold and damp night - but I do believe he wouldn't care if we were seen. His lips hit mine with such force my head snaps back and I bump it on the far side door.

He just kisses me. Hard and insistent, his tongue pressing forward, moving against my own, showing that he is in charge. I kiss back with passion. I cannot help myself: this man who smells so clean and rich, this man who I barely know, this man who pays me for sex is irresistible.

His kisses dip down to my neck; he bites and I hiss, my fingers digging into his arms in shock. He continues down, licking, kissing, and biting and setting my whole body alight. I know I shouldn't want him to arouse me - if he doesn't, I get double the money - but my body just can't help but respond to his dominant kisses and his commanding caresses.

He pulls my breasts from their confines, pulls them up and out and sucks on each nipple with gusto.

'I've wanted to taste your tits for so long,' he says between mouthfuls, 'and they're so fucking tasty.'

I can't help myself. I mewl and purr with pleasure as he mauls my breasts. I love rough sex and my breasts feel best when they spill out around squeezing fingers. A cold wind tickles my thigh and reminds me of where I am, in public being fucked by a near stranger. I tilt my hips, I can't help it; I'm hot and desperate for him, my cunt aches to be filled. I rub against the lump in his trousers and moan.

Without speaking, one hand drops to his pants. I hear the zip and a second later I feel his head rubbing between my slick lips.

'You hot bitch,' he hisses, 'already soaking fucking wet. You're such a slut, a fucking beautiful slut.'

He slams his cock into me, one leg on the floor of the car, the other on the seat. He pulls on my hips, angling me so he can thrust in all the deeper. My head keeps hitting the doorframe but I don't care; his cock is inside me, he's fucking me, and he's paid for the pleasure. I'm so horny I want to reach down and frig myself to orgasm but I can't, he's got to make me come and I'm not going to make it easy for him.

'Fuck, I can't last much longer,' he gasps, my heart sinking slightly, 'You're too fucking hot to handle.'

'Told you I was the best,' I reply, linking my arms around his neck and running my fingers through his hair.

'You didn't lie.' He growls and bites down on my neck, hard. I howl out in pain and pleasure and he pumps his come into me. I'm close, so close, right on the edge but no orgasm yet. I've won.

'You owe me another five grand.' It's my time to smirk, even if my cunt is throbbing with need.

'Oh, I've not finished with you yet.' He slips out of me and pushes me up into the corner so I'm sitting up, my legs still spread. 'I want to return the favour from this morning.'

His hand sweeps down my body and slips into my cunt. His fingers thrust in and out, mixing our juices inside me, releasing the scent of sex to mingle on the air with damp grass and warm leather.

'Do you like that, slut?' he whispers against my ear, his body pressed into me.

'Yes,' I reply as his thumb seeks out my clit.

'Yes, what?'

'Yes, sir.' My pussy contracts with pleasure.

'That's better. You're mine, whore. I've paid for you, you'll show me due respect.'

'Yes, sir.' The orgasm is building inside me, bubbling and boiling, eager to break free.

'You're my whore, you're my delicious slut and I'm going to make you come all over my fucking fingers. You're going to drown them in your juices as you imagine my cock in your mouth, in your cunt, in your arse. You're going to cream as you think of what a dirty thing you're doing. Fucking me, a stranger for cash.'

I am going to come; my chest is flushed, my breaths are ragged, and my eyes are tightly closed.

'Look at me slut.' I do and I am lost in his lustful stare. 'Now come for me.'

I don't know if he just reads my body signs right or if his command makes me come but I explode then, juices gushing over his fingers and down my thighs. I grasp on to him and scream into his shoulder, my body shuddering, sweat beading on my brow.

I slip back, panting, as he extricates his fingers and licks them one by one.

'As arousing as this is,' he says between licks, 'I believe it may work out cheaper if I ask you out on a date and we do this the proper way.'

'I wouldn't count on it,' I reply. 'I could really go for a big steak right about now.'

I laugh and he joins in, the laughter lines showing around his eyes, softening his look for the first time since I met him.

'Right, steaks it is, only the best for my slut. The best slut in the north.'

Mean
by Maxim Jakubowski

I gift myself to men.

That's what I do.

Call me what you will: slut, whore, irresponsible, crazy, masochist, nymphomaniac, fuckmeat, whatever, and you won't see me raising much in the way of objections.

It's in my nature, you see, and I have learnt, for good or for bad, that there is little I can do about it. I've tried, I assure you. On many occasions. It's not something I take lightly. I have wrestled with my conscience, battled with my soul until both of us were defeated by technical knock-out, debated endlessly with my heart.

I am what I am (didn't Popeye the sailor man originally say that?).

I crave the cocks of men, more often than not those of total strangers; I hunger for their wrath, their hardness, the punishment they mercilessly inflict upon me. It's not their faces that draw me towards them, or their feelings, or their love, it's the multi-shape and size and length of their cocks that I seek, like a mad pilgrim, in my adventures in the fuck trade. The anonymity of their penises.

There are many names for women like me. None shocks me. None is insulting. Not a single one hurts me where it counts.

I am submissive.

That's what I am.

* * *

I'd passed seamlessly from rebellious and curious teenage experiments through the mild promiscuousness of university years to a gentler patchwork of almost monogamous relationships in my twenties. It seemed to be the way things should be, as I observed my contemporaries with wry detachment and saw how my life's itinerary followed a similar pattern and the hollowness of absence began to carve its deep-etched hole inside me. Was this all there was to it? Small epiphanies followed by gentle joys, ups and downs, maybe one day "the one" and ensuing domestic calm, children maybe? Surely life should consist of more, no? And normal sex was grandly overrated once you'd got the hang of it. Vanilla as I'd soon learn it was called.

Men kept coming and going. Some lasted. Others didn't stay for coffee the morning after. A few I lived with. And some were nice, pleasing, affectionate, husband material even. Two even proposed.

But, at the end of the day, it was just the mechanics of sex and quiet companionship, and an insistent small voice inside was telling me that I wanted, needed more. Something.

To cut a short story short, I met this man.

Older.

Married.

Not available.

And because both of us knew there was no future in it, somehow the sex was better than usual; it was good. Electric. The sort of sex that reminds you what it is to be alive.

We met in hotel rooms, in basements, business offices, and the clandestine nature of the sort of relationship we were having awakened the cravings I had such difficulty keeping a lid on. And because we were so tuned to each other, we had that telepathy that comes of the communion of sweat and semen and inner juices, he sensed it.

One night, a few stolen hours, on the carpeted floor of his

office, him inside me, thrusting, adjusting the rhythms of our lust until they matched in perfect fuck unison, I opened my eyes and looked into his. Brown, a hazy close-up.

Maybe it was the way I looked at him, silently, but so full of unsaid words (I've always been told that my eyes always look sort of glazed once I've been fucked, an unmistakable identifying sign).

An involuntary signal.

Triggering something buried deep inside him.

Cause and effect.

As his body pressed down against mine, his hands slowly moved away from holding my buttocks in their firm grasp, pulling my midriff closer to him as we often did when we had sex, to deepen the penetration in the missionary position (not my favourite one, but you have to vary, don't you?).

His hands moved to my neck.

Settled on my jugular.

Then, interrogation in his eyes, me still squirming and moaning quietly beneath him, he began pressing.

Mad thoughts raced through my brain. Illogical, desperate, surely not? Harder. His thumbs no doubt creating deep indents into the smooth, white flesh of my neck. Jesus! How far would he go? How much harder would he press? A jumble of frantic and conflicting emotions was bubbling away through my grey cells, and my blood felt as if was about to reach boiling point.

I took a deep breath, idly thinking it was going to be my last. Storing up the oxygen or whatever I needed to keep alive, for my lungs to feed on.

I came with all the ferocity of nuclear resonance.

Couldn't recall such a powerful orgasm. Ever.

Still impaled on him, my body convulsing in rapidly diminishing waves, I felt his fingers move away from my neck. The caress of his breath against my skin as he exhaled.

A mad thought occurred: would my skin show bruises? (In fact it didn't, the pressure had actually been very mild …)

Later, I asked him, as we bathed in post-coital languor, 'If I'd kept on being silent, would you have continued pressing against my neck?'

'No, of course,' he said. 'No way.'

'Why did you do it?'

'Not sure. You had that look on your face, you know. As if inviting me to do terrible things … Can't explain it.'

'Did I?'

'Absolutely. What did it feel like?'

'Felt so vulnerable, as if everything was out of my control. Both scared and excited.'

At home that night, in bed, my mind anywhere but absorbed by the pages of the novel I was reading, the realisation came to me. Why I had been so affected by my lover's uncommon and unexpected gesture.

The danger, the possibility of being hurt, damaged in some way, had whispered to me and I had responded. I had been introduced to a whole new world. Of the mind. Of the senses.

Whenever the subject of BDSM had reared its head previously during the course of my sexual life, it was something I had airily dismissed. I had no taste for spanking, either as spanker or spankee, and found the whole thing somewhat odd. Fancy getting kicks from pain, albeit mild! And then there was all the paraphernalia of the sub/dom scene: the leather, the latex, the toys, the ridiculous implements, the outdated rituals, more a subject for mirth than pleasure in my opinion.

And the fact I had never even been in the slightest bit curious about it surely meant that it wasn't for me.

The next time we met, I said, 'Again …'

He did.

Yet later, I suggested he hurt me. And not just a spanking.

Then, 'Tie me up.'

One step at a time, boundary after boundary passed, I realised what I was, the roots of my submission crawled to the surface and I assumed my nature. I was on the downward path but I knew it was the right road to take.

Eventually, we parted.

None of the men who came after him, in my bed, in theirs, in my life, showed the same understanding of what I was, what I craved for. So, they came and went.

I would have to fill my needs in different ways.

I stormed the Internet. Chatrooms, alt groups, Craigslist. Ventured to private clubs, parties, confidential and shady events, fetish nights (for which I had to force myself to wear a modicum of leather; tastefully at any rate …).

Learned my ABC.

Made bad mistakes.

Discovered more of what moved me, made me tick.

See, I did not wish to become anyone's sub. Had no need for a full-time dom, or master or whatever they wanted you call them. I had no wish to be owned, or kept. I had a good job, earned above the average, had my own flat and a mortgage whose repayments were well under control, even had a small nest egg for possible rainy days. What more could a gal ask?

When I advertised my availability I presented myself as "unowned". My way of being a freelance submissive, so to speak!

I wanted to be used. With no strings attached. Rough. Hard. Humiliatingly. Sometimes even degraded. (I'm still to truly appreciate the joys of golden showers, though.)

It mattered not that many of the men who took me up on the offer were men I wouldn't go near with a barge pole in normal, social circumstances. They were not men: they were just cocks, anonymous wills to which I bended, because that's what made me whole.

I was there to be used.

Even now, I still cannot remember any of their faces. The faceless men. The fuckers. The tops. The doms. The would-be masters.

But I can evoke with crystal-like clarity the comforting solidity of their thighs, the squareness of their shoulders, the basso profundo of their voices as they instructed me, ordered me, threatened me, mounted me. Sometimes it was in the privacy of a bedroom or a clearing in a forest or on the floor at a special party with onlookers watching their cocks fill me, stretch me, gaping me.

There are occasions when it's all rather scary and I shudder, wondering if I will get out of the scene alive, unharmed, unmarked. But living on the edge is just such a special feeling. There are no words for it.

It can hurt and not always be pleasurable at the time, when the fear takes over and I have to concentrate on the situation rather than my own, selfish pleasure. But little old me is there, recording it all, for posterity, for the privacy of my mental screenings on later occasions.

But sometimes I come and the radiance of ecstasy spreads out like radiation from the pit of my loins and it's like the brightness of an atomic sun, and it surprises me that it doesn't contaminate the whole, surrounding room, and cut every voyeur and onlooker dead on the spot, so harsh is the energy released from my moans, my silent screams, my riding of the lust waves, the surfer on the sea of sex that I have become.

Or that the hotel room in which I am being mounted does not catch fire, bedding, curtains, bathroom towels and all, in the same way that the fire within is burning so fiercely inside my body, my head, my heart, my cunt.

Other times, I don't come at all. Maybe it's the geometry of the locale, the wrong Feng Shui, the alignment of the planets, but still, the way I'm filled to the hilt by the unknown cocks of unknown men, the rough way I'm handled (oh yes, they can be very rough indeed), the verbal insults, all that stays in my mind for days, weeks on end, and I can drag those feelings and memories up from the depths at will whenever I need that kick again, when I am alone in my bed, or in my glass-windowed office, and then I come on demand, properly.

There is a subtle difference between being submissive to men and being a slave and, were I not so independent, I might be the latter.

I look at pictures on Tumblr, on sites hosted by doms and subs and masters and slaves, and I picture myself in all the obscene poses and situations, some of which I have actually experienced.

I must confess I am tempted.

I once attended an Erotic Ball of some sort in a draughty warehouse by the Thames, overlooking the Millennium Dome across the river, and was struck by the vision of a cloaked, grey-haired man in his fifties leading a beautiful young woman on a leash attached to a black leather studded collar surrounding her throat and parading her through the room. All she wore was a blindfold and tasty high-heeled pumps (Christian Louboutin, I think). Her back was so straight. Her skin shone. There was some jewellery shining between her legs, a piercing of some kind, her arse was so round and perfect and I remember that her breasts were rather small, not unlike mine, although the colouring of her nipples was much redder (maybe lipstick?). For a moment, I wished I could be her. I wanted to follow them and see where he was taking her and what fate he had in mind for his pet, but there was a crowd and it somehow felt inappropriate right then and I never saw the couple again for the rest of the evening.

Could I become a slave?

Owned by just one man.

He would have to know me well, know which buttons to press.

Just the thought makes me wet.

Property.

Trained.

With no control over anything any longer.

Pierced under his command.

Infibulated like O.

The tattoo of a barcode across my left buttock.

Oh Jesus, what I am thinking of?

Surely not, but then …

My lips feel dry. The heat inside my cunt feels like a furnace, the ants in my stomach are dancing the light fantastic. I sigh. I take a deep breath. Brush my fringe away from my forehead. I'm sweating.

Is this the inevitable next step? My mind is racing.

I take a sip of cold water straight from the tap.

Return to the desk and open the laptop.

Boot up.

Log on.

Find those sites I'd bookmarked out of sheer curiosity some time ago.

Collarme.com

Slavefarm.com

Auctionhouse.net

There's an embarrassment of choices.

I click.

Enter my universal password (the first name of the man who first put his fingers around my neck and switched me on).

Type.

Unowned sub/would-be slave in London seeks to be trained, used, abused. Late 20s, blonde, tall, slim, 34A, shaven, long legs, arse slightly too large. No limits.

Enter.

Wait.

There's not long to wait and the offers come rushing in.

Sir2U <OK, I've received your pics. You will do nicely>

  Cornelia <Thank u, sir>

  Sir2U <I will give u a trial>

  Cornelia <OK>

  Sir2U <You will come to the address I give you and from the moment you pass the door, I will own you fully>

  Cornelia <I understand, sir>

  Sir2U <You will not wear any underwear>

  Cornelia <I never wear a bra anyway, sir. Not too opulent ... >

  Sir2U <So I see in the photos you submitted. Small is good. No limits?>

  Cornelia <No, sir>

  Sir2U < You will be thoroughly used in all holes. No will not be accepted as an answer>

  Cornelia <Yes, sir>

  Sir2U <You have experience of anal?>

  Cornelia <Yes sir, although am often told I am still quite tight there>

  Sir2U <Perfect. We'll soon see that you are more welcoming there, girl>

  Cornelia <Yes, sir>

  Sir2U <Good slut>

  Cornelia <Thank you, sir>

  Sir2U <And you agree to be shared with other tops, whenever I order you to do so?>

  Cornelia <Yes, sir>

  Sir2U <Ever been gangbanged?>

  Cornelia <No, sir, not technically, although have on a few occasions been with more than one man>

  Sir2U <Liked it?>

  Cornelia <I am a sub. It's not for me to like or dislike, sir>

  Sir2U <Excellent answer. You'll go far. You will be trained, moulded, restrained whenever I wish, broken to my will>

Cornelia <Yes, sir>

Sir2U <Punished when I deem it necessary ...>

Cornelia <I understand, sir>

Sir2U <You will be at my beck and call. I can summon you at any time I chose>

Cornelia <Well, sir, I have a job and ...>

Sir2U <OK, but I will nonetheless expect total obedience and there will be severe punishment for any occasions when you cannot make yourself available>

Cornelia <OK, sir>

Sir2U <What sort of work do you, slave?>

Cornelia <In media, sir>

Sir2U <Very good. Then, in addition to being my slave whore, you can also be my cash slave and pay me tributes>

Cornelia <Tributes?>

Sir2U <I'll be reasonable, but you must pay for your upkeep. In cash or gifts to your master>

Cornelia <?>

Sir2U <What?>

Cornelia <Fuck no ...>

I disconnect, bile rising up through my throat.

The damn bastard wants me to pay for the privilege of being fucked and used. Surely, it should be the other way around?

The suggestion sickens me.

If he'd suggested pimping me, auctioning me, slave trading me (and now you know how dark and filthy my mind and cravings are ...) and pocketing the proceeds, I would somehow not have objected. But this is different.

No way.

No fucking way.

Damn!

Call me a slut, a whore or whatever word you feel is appropriate for my failings and I will not be offended.

Because deep down I know that I am all those things and more.

So now, there you are, you now can add yet another word to the thesaurus that is me.

Call me mean.

Party Favour
by Catelyn Cash

'I've told you! I'm not a stripper!'

The men looked at each other; looked at Maya. 'You look like a stripper,' said one.

Maya glared. In truth, dressed in a basque and a ridiculous, frilly skirt, she did look like a stripper. 'I'm a singing telegram. There's a difference.'

The speaker reached into his pocket for his wallet. 'How much of a difference?'

She glared again but spoiled the affect by letting her eyes stray to the money in his hand. Holy crap. Obviously strippers got paid way better than singing telegrams. 'I'm not a stripper,' she said again, less forcefully.

There was a small group of men gathered in the hotel suite for the stag party and they were all staring at her. One of them stepped forward and Maya couldn't believe she had missed him before. Dark hair and blue eyes; her favourite combination. Mouth-wateringly gorgeous. 'Hi. I'm Rick. You do work for Party Time?'

'Party *Favour*,' she corrected, hoping she wasn't drooling, faced with so much male beauty.

Rick turned to the man with the wallet. 'Looks like you rang the wrong company. Did you specifically ask for a stripper?'

'I asked for someone who does extras,' the first man said defensively.

They all looked at Maya again. 'I do extras.' She nodded

vigorously. 'I dance.'

She was dressed in a can can outfit, cheap and tacky. Rick took her by the elbow and led her to one side. 'The thing is, my friend's getting married tomorrow. That's why we requested the extras. Maybe we can come to some arrangement?'

He smelled gorgeous, and Maya consciously had to stop herself sniffing him. She would like to come to an arrangement with him. *Oh yeah.* 'I'm paid to sing, not take my clothes off.'

'No?' He gave her a smile she felt all the way to her toes. 'I'd pay to see you take your clothes off,' he said softly.

To her horror Maya felt her nipples harden and heat flood her pussy. She searched his face for signs he was taking the mickey but there were none. Which was crazy. She wasn't the sort of woman men paid to see naked. Far too many curves, way too much bounce.

'Look.' He indicated a pile of money on the table and, though she tried hard not to be, Maya was impressed. 'We had a whip round for the stripper,' he explained.

She licked her lips. That amount of money would pay her rent for the rest of the month.

'It's yours. If you strip.'

Her excitement faded. The money would be great but the idea of taking her clothes off in front of these men brought her out in a cold sweat. 'Your friends might pay me to keep my clothes on,' she said, trying for a joke.

'Meaning?' He frowned.

'Well, unless you're paying by the pound, I'm not exactly stripper material.'

'Who told you that?'

'My last boyfriend would have preferred me to wear a burqa in public,' she admitted. 'He hated his friends looking at me.'

Rick eyed her impressive cleavage. 'He must have been the jealous type.'

She laughed. 'Smooth, but no deal. Do you want me to deliver the telegram? It's a really catchy tune.'

'What would it take for you to save my friend's stag night?'

'A weight loss of two stone.'

'You're kidding. You don't like your body? That's why you won't strip?'

Wasn't that reason enough? 'Bingo.'

His blue gaze narrowed speculatively. 'So you've nothing against stripping in principle?'

She laughed again. If she had the body for it she would walk naked down the High Street just to show it off.

'What if I told you have the most sensuous body I've seen in years?'

The way he was looking at her, Maya could almost believe him. In fact, the way he was looking at her sent another rush of heat to her groin. 'Then I'd assume you'd just got out of prison.'

He turned to the waiting men. 'Who wants to see the can can girl strip?'

There were cheers and catcalls and whistles.

'See,' he said. 'They want to see you. A few of them might want to do more.'

'Is that what you mean by extras? Your stripper was going to … to have sex with you? With all of you?' Her voice had risen to a squeak at the very idea. But her pussy clenched excitedly.

Rick's gaze never left her face. 'You like the sound of that, don't you?'

She shook her head, unconvincingly.

'Liar,' he murmured. 'What's your name?

'Maya.'

'Well Maya, the "extras" were a little show she was going to put on for us. First she was going to strip. Then she was going to masturbate while we watched.'

Heat shot through her and she thought bloody hell!

'People actually do that?'

'The question is, do you?'

'Strip naked and bring myself off in front of a load of strangers? I think not.'

He grinned again and she felt her pussy clench. 'Come on. You like that idea. In fact you're getting turned on. So am I. I can picture you, touching yourself, sliding your fingers inside your pussy. I'll watch you and wish it was my cock. My tongue. I'll watch you and all I will think about is fucking you.'

Her nipples tightened at his words and Rick noticed. 'I want to see your tits too. To watch you suck on your nipples. Can you do that?'

She nodded, mesmerised. No tiny titties for her. Instead she had big, swollen mammas that were tingling inside her basque.

'This is turning you on,' said Rick. 'Admit it. The thought of spreading your legs for us is getting you going. Every cock in the room will be standing for you. Men will go home and fuck their wives tonight thinking of you.'

God, she was almost coming on the spot at the image he conjured up. Maya looked over at the other men and saw there were already some bulges in their trousers.

'I'm not having sex with anyone.' Had she really said that?

'Of course not. Pleasure yourself and the money is yours.'

Maya knew she was going to agree; knew she would explode if she didn't have an orgasm soon. 'And I'm not getting naked,' she warned.

'Fine. Do what you're comfortable with. But we see your tits. And your pussy.'

She could do that. It was her less than flat belly she wanted to hide. 'So …?'

Rick indicated a wide cream leather sofa. 'Over there. If you sit or lie there we can see everything.'

Maya wasn't a stripper; she had no idea how to perform. Unable to believe she had agreed to this, she walked unsteadily across the room. Self-consciously, and keeping her back to the men, she started to undress.

The skirt was first. Cheap and frilly, it was easy to dispose of. Underneath she wore a red and black basque and fishnet hold-ups. A thong, because the nylon netting on the skirt was so hot. Still with her back to the room, she hooked her fingers into the elastic and, taking a deep breath, she yanked the thong off. She heard a ripple of appreciation and realised a dozen men were staring her bare bottom. Heat rushed through her and she quickly pulled the basque down, allowing her boobs to pop out. She heard a murmur and saw that a couple of the men had circled round and were gazing at her breasts. When they caught her eye they raised their glasses in salute.

'Fucking great tits,' one of them said appreciatively. I'd love to slide my cock between them.'

'Bill,' said a warning voice and she knew it was Rick.

The other man grinned sheepishly. 'Sorry. But great tits anyway.'

There was such genuine admiration in his voice it gave her the courage to turn and face the others. She stood there, face flaming, while a bunch of strange men ogled her. Think of the money, she reminded herself. Think of paying your rent without having to sing stupid telegrams. But what she was really thinking of was cocks stirring in trousers. Were they getting hard? Was it possible Rick was right and they found her body a turn-on?

'Sit down on the sofa.'

Glad of some instruction she obeyed Rick's command. 'Lie back.' She did that too; felt her breasts wobble.

'Real,' whispered someone. 'Have to be real.'

Her nipples were like organ stops, swollen and hard. She couldn't resist. Lifting her hands, she brushed them over each tip and felt a jolt of pleasure between her thighs.

'That's right, Maya, touch yourself. Pull on your nipples,' coaxed Rick. 'We're all wishing we could suck on them.' She lifted them obligingly and sucked gently, first one, then the other, moaning softly. There was another low, murmur around the room. 'Now open your legs. Let us see you.'

By now Maya was so turned on she couldn't have refused if she wanted to. All she could think of was the men watching her, cocks getting harder. For her. Eyes closed, she did as instructed and was embarrassed by the musky tang of sex that immediately surrounded her.

'Touch yourself,' said Rick and his voice had grown husky. 'Between your legs. Show us what you do when you're alone.'

She wanted to open her eyes. She wanted to see how close they were but didn't dare. They wouldn't be masturbating, not in public, but maybe there were a few hands in pockets, maybe they were touching themselves, keeping their cocks hard. She slid a hand down her belly, through her damp curls, parting her outer lips. The room was silent now as she dipped her finger into her pussy, swirled it gently in the slick moisture she found there before circling her clit with her finger. It felt great and she sighed. Normally she needed the help of her vibrator to achieve orgasm but something told her that wasn't going to be necessary tonight.

Still picturing her audience, she decided to put on a show. She pushed a finger inside, deeper this time, rubbing her thumb over her clit, bringing herself close but staying on edge. She teased her nipple with one hand, her other hand working her pussy hard, her fingers flashing, moving fast, then slowing down, prolonging the pleasure. Her head was lashing from side to side and she could hear soft moans, knew they were coming from her. The pleasure built, and built, and then she was coming, her hips lifting off the sofa, her thighs clamping round her hand as she cried out. As she slowly sank back down to earth, she heard the men's murmured appreciation but didn't open her eyes, knowing that she would be embarrassed now it was over. She'd stay here until they were gone, grab her money, and run. Don't open your eyes. Don't open your eyes.

'Open your eyes.'

She did. Most of the men had gone but Rick was still there as she had somehow known he would be. And two of the other men too. She sat up, eying them warily. 'I'll be off, then.'

'What's the hurry?'

The hurry was she felt incredibly self-conscious sitting here half-naked under their scrutiny. She tried not to look at their crotches, wondered if they were as randy as she was. 'I'm done, aren't I?'

'If you want to be. But if you want a bit more …'

'What do you mean?'

'A game,' Rick proposed. 'With the three of us.'

She licked her lips. 'What kind of game?'

He glanced at his companions. 'We want to fuck you.'

Her eyes widened. 'All of you?'

'All of us,' he confirmed. 'Repeatedly. We want to fuck you and we'll pay for the privilege.'

'Are you serious? You think I'm going to let all three of you …'

'Fuck you?' he said helpfully and her face flushed. So did her pussy.

'Yes. I mean no. I mean what do you think I am?'

'I think you're the sexiest woman I have ever seen. I think your pussy is a thing of beauty and I can't wait to slide my cock into it. I want my cock between your lips too. And your tits.'

The other men nodded eagerly.

'We'll pay.' Rick pulled out a bank note and she saw it was a fifty.

They were going to pay her £50 for sex? She had no idea

60

what the going rate was for fucking strangers. 'Each?' she blurted.

He smiled, knowing he had her. 'Per orgasm. Ours, not yours.'

She did a quick calculation. Three of them. Maybe two orgasms each. Three hundred pounds. Bloody hell. Add that to what she already had and she could give up singing telegrams for the rest of term, actually study for her exams.

'In fact, I'll double the money every time you make one of us come. But just to make it more interesting, you can't come yourself.'

'What?'

'You can't come. If you do, you lose half of what's in the pot. How's that?'

Make them come as often as she could? The idea excited her like crazy. She could have one cock in each hand and one in her mouth. And she didn't need to worry about not coming herself. One orgasm was the norm for her and she'd already had that.

'Deal,' she said quickly wondering how long it had been since she'd stood in front of them and announced, archly, 'I'm not a stripper.'

Rick smiled. 'I just have one more condition. You have to have your hands tied. I'm not having you jerk us off too quickly.'

She grinned back, knowing he had read her mind. 'You expect me to let three strange men tie me up and fuck me? Seriously?'

'We won't hurt you. The hotel staff saw you come in and your firm knows you're here.'

True. Anyway, she was so hot by this time, she wasn't going to say no. 'You pay every time one of you comes. I come, I lose half.'

He nodded. 'That way we get your very best attention. And you have an incentive to keep the session going as long as you can.

'Done.'

The word was barely out of her mouth when the other two men were naked. Rick tied her hands behind her back with one of their neckties. To her horror, he also unhooked her basque and let it fall to the floor. She had nothing on but her stay-up fishnets and in seconds they were gone too. 'Wait a minute,' she began but no one was listening.

The first man gently pushed her down onto the sofa. He gathered her boobs in his hands and fervently rubbed his cock along the deep furrow between them. Maya looked down at the gleaming cockhead as it slid backwards and forwards. If she only had her hands free, she could touch him ...

'Fuck!' He gasped, coming explosively over her chest, and she had no idea who was more surprised, him or her.

'Sorry,' he muttered. 'You have no idea how turned on I was watching you frig yourself.'

'No problem,' she said, bemused that a man could be so excited by her body. *Her* body. He took out some money and slapped it down on the table. A hundred quid now. Wow.

The next man sat down beside her. 'What about a blowjob?'

With enthusiasm but some difficulty considering her bound hands, she knelt between his legs. Maya loved sucking cock and she was good at it. The next hundred was almost hers and she grinned up at him before sliding her lips down his length. He was big enough that she had to stretch her lips and she closed her eyes in bliss, then opened them as she felt a touch between her legs.

Rick was kneeling behind her, naked, and though she couldn't see his cock, she could feel it, velvet-covered steel against her cheeks as he reached round and fondled her boobs. She groaned deep in her throat and lost her rhythm a little, suddenly realising this might not be the cakewalk she had thought. Rick's hands on her boobs were magic, and when she felt his cock glide over her clit she felt that first tingle and knew she was in trouble. *Concentrate*, she told herself, concentrate on the cock in her mouth, make him come. Please come before Rick's big cock went into her, because she didn't know if would be able to hold off her orgasm then.

She groaned again as she felt him slide along her slick lips. She sucked deeply on the cock, took it all the way, working him with her tongue. Make him come, make him come, make him come. And all the while Rick touched and stroked, touched and stroked.

She whimpered, the sound vibrating deep in her throat and suddenly the man fucking her mouth gasped and she almost choked as thick jets of come hit the back of her throat. Swallowing quickly, she licked him clean, all the while anticipating the delicious slide of Rick's cock into her cunt.

It didn't happen. Instead, Rick flipped her over and lifted her onto the sofa. Her hands were pinned behind her but she barely noticed the discomfort. Noticed only the head between her legs, his blue eyes as he winked up at her.

'Two down. But I'm not so easy.' He lowered his mouth and she almost lifted off the sofa as he parted her lips with his tongue, tasting every bit of her. Maya clenched her teeth. She wasn't going to come. Not yet. Hell no. She had only just begun.

But Rick really knew what he was doing. And one of the other men was sucking on her nipple, taking it deep into his mouth, and she was thrashing and groaning. This was terrible. She was going to come before Rick. She moaned and writhed, losing the battle.

But so was Rick. Swearing, he grabbed a condom, slipped it on and rammed into her.

Her triumph lasted only seconds. Her control slipped away again as he thrust into her, hard and fast. She could feel his impeding orgasm but could feel hers too. She fought against it but he was going deep, going really deep …

'Oh fuck,' Rick gasped.

His entire body stiffened as he emptied himself into her, his cock pulsing wildly. Part of her was grinning in triumph while another part of her screamed in frustration.

Rick rolled away and laughed aloud as he dropped more money down on the table.

Maya barely had time to gloat when the first man, already hard again, settled between her legs. The condom was on and her pussy was slick and primed as he guided himself into her. Not as big as Rick, not as thick. But he built up a really nice rhythm as he held her legs wide and pounded her clit with each thrust and, worryingly, she felt her orgasm building again. He sensed it too and gave her a wicked grin. She squeezed her pussy muscles, gripping him tightly. Next moment, unbelievably, he was coming again, like a train, gasping and grinding.

Maya laughed in delight. She couldn't believe she was doing this, couldn't believe she had so much power over them, even with her hands tied. And with every orgasm the pile of money on the table grew higher.

Before she could even begin to count it she was picked up by strong arms and deposited directly onto a rigid cock. Sitting astride the second man's lap she struggled for balance, especially with her hands tied but she managed it by leaning forward and soon saw he was almost hypnotised by her breasts swinging so close to his face. 'Oh fuck,' he kept saying, as he thrust up into her. 'Oh fucking hell.'

Power surged through Maya as she realised he was going to come again. On a roll, she looked for another cock. Didn't have to look far. 'In my mouth,' she commanded. 'Fuck my mouth.'

The man ramming into her kicked up the beat as he watched her take a cock into her mouth and suck on it greedily. She would have these two off before they knew it. And it felt so good. Maybe then she would allow herself the orgasm that was so close.

She rode one cock, ate another, and didn't wonder where Rick was until she felt him, felt his hand on her bum, felt something press against her backside. She let the cock slip from her mouth as her head whipped round.

'What the …?'

Rick leant over her and whispered in her ear. 'I'm going to make you come,' he promised. She felt his finger, slick and warm, and she realised he had poured lube over her.

'What are you doing?' she demanded, panic rising.

'This.' His finger circled, pushed, circled, pushed and finally the puckered rim of her anus gave, and it slipped inside. Maya's entire body stilled as she concentrated on this whole knew sensation. 'You want me to stop?' Rick whispered.

'No,' she admitted, shaking all over.

He bit her ear. 'Are you going to come?'

'No.' She gritted her teeth.

'Not even with my cock in you too? Three cocks in you?' He signalled the man at her head and he slid his cock back between her parted lips and she sucked instinctively. The cock in her pussy was still moving slowly but her entire focus was on Rick and what he was doing. Having relaxed her with his finger, he now slowly, slowly, pushed his cock into her tight passage. 'Take it,' he murmured in her ear. 'We just have to go slow. How does that feel?'

She couldn't speak; her eyes were closed in bliss as one man pumped her pussy and another fucked her mouth The guy in her mouth was close and she felt his seed gather at the base, felt it shoot along his shaft and straight down her throat. Another one, she thought, dizzily. And then she was lost to sensation as she was fucked, fore and aft, the two men setting up a rhythm. A rhythm of pure pleasure.

Maya didn't care about the money now, didn't care about anything, could only focus on the sensations building, building inside her. She heard the man beneath her gasp, felt

65

the searing heat of his orgasm, felt a moment of triumph that she had outlasted him but there was no way she could fight it a moment longer.

She gave herself over to sensation as waves of intense pleasure burst through her, bathing her, drowning her. She was keening like an animal, the sound wild and feral, and she jammed herself down on the two cocks. A second later she heard Rick yell as he slid all the way in, holding himself still as he shot deep into her virgin hole.

She'd come before him. She'd lost half the money but she didn't care. How could she after an orgasm like that?

Gentle hands lifted her as though she weighed nothing and she felt herself lowered down onto Rick's lap. He held her in his arms and stroked her thigh, while her body twitched with delicious little aftershocks.

'You're wasted as a singing telegram.'

'Maybe. But I'm pretty sure professional sex workers don't come. Or not so noisily.'

'Well, you're new at it,' he assured her. 'Maybe you just need practice.'

She opened her eyes; looked into his bright blue ones. 'What do you mean?'

'I mean I've another friend getting married next week. Another stag party.'

A slow smile split his face and she grinned back at the very idea of doing this all over again. 'Make sure you tell him I do extras.'

Creamed
by Landon Dixon

I began to question the whole point of belonging to a fraternity when I was instructed to jerk off into the Dean's morning cup of coffee as part of my initiation.

Emilio Rodriguez took me aside and explained it to me. 'The Dean's secretary always brings him a fresh cup of coffee first thing in the morning. All you have to do is hang around outside the Dean's office while I phone in a distraction, and then slip right on inside and jack off into his coffee. Nothing to it.'

The tall, thin, creamed-coffee-coloured frat brother threw an arm around my shoulder and grinned down at me, full of confidence – that I was going to be caught and expelled, no doubt. 'Uh, can't I just kidnap Benny the Beaver and let him loose in the zoology department's boreal forest exhibit?' I asked. Benny the Beaver was the mascot for the school's football team, the Snapping Beavers.

'No dice, pledge,' Emilio replied happily, squeezing my shoulder encouragingly. 'You do this and you won't have to do anything else during pledge week. Not a bad deal, huh?'

'Couldn't I just spit in the Dean's coffee?' I persisted. Even with my hair-trigger hand and cock, jerking off was going to take some time, leaving me exposed in more ways than one.

Emilio's arm slipped off my shoulder, the good-looking guy's brown eyes going from soft to hard. 'You bucking a frat brother's command, pledge?'

My shoulders slumped without the support. 'No,' I groaned.

The Dean's office was located in the 200-year-old administrative building which had formerly been the college itself, before expansion. He was up on the third floor; his office opened up at 8.30 a.m. I was outside in the hall at 8 a.m., wearing a pair of sweatpants and no underpants for quick and easy access and a guilty as hell expression on my freckled face.

A man came trotting down the hall towards the Dean's door, and I turned and scrupulously studied the painting of the first Dean, Rev. Harding Manners, on the wall opposite. From the corner of my nervous grey eyes, I saw the man pull a key out of his pocket, stick it in the lock, and open the door.

He went inside, shutting the door after him. I glanced up and down the shiny, empty hallway, my dick as scared as the rest of me, then pushed the door open and went on through.

The Dean's outer office was small and formal, carpeted in blood-red, dark wood panelling on the walls. There were three hard-backed wooden chairs, a desk where the man with the key was standing. He was darker than the wood, mahogany in colour, short and slim and fine-featured, with brown eyes and black hair, dressed in a pair of dark-blue slacks and a white dress shirt and a blue blazer. He sort of looked like Carlton from *The Fresh Prince of Bel-Air*, only thinner and less obnoxious.

'Can I help you?' he asked.

His voice was as cultivated as his manner. 'Um, yeah, I wanted to see the Dean.'

He gave me the once-over. My sweatpants and T-shirt seemed woefully out of place, like the whole crazy scheme. 'Do you have an appointment?'

'N-no!' I gulped.

'Well, you have to have an appointment. The Dean's a very busy man, you know.'

'Oh, OK!' I turned and wrestled with the polished brass doorknob, which kept slipping out of my sweaty hand. There were plenty of other fraternities on campus. Hazing seemed like a welcome prospect.

'If it's really important, the Dean *might* be able to see you right at 8.30, first thing when he comes in.'

I barely heard the guy. Why the hell didn't he just let me flee? 'Oh, OK,' I mouthed, staring at the heavy, dark wood of the door.

'You can sit down and wait, if you like,' Andrew said after a minute or so.

That was his name – Andrew Cole. I got that off his brass nameplate when I finally got my muscles working again and turned around. I stiff-legged it over to a chair, folded myself down into it. Andrew smiled coolly at me. I blushed back, as I told him my name was Rufus Nerdlinger. I didn't think good under pressure.

The minutes dragged by like a public affairs lecture, my brief college career flashing before my eyes. Was coming in someone's coffee vandalism, assault, or an act of terrorism? Why the hell hadn't I taken a Viagra or something, arrived with an already loaded pair of pants?

The hands on the grandfather clock in the corner trembled arthritically around to 8.30, and at that exact instant, the outer door burst open and the Dean of the university stormed in. I just about jumped up out of my chair and through the window in behind Andrew.

'Good morning, Dean Skinner,' the cool and composed assistant said to his boss.

'Morning, Andrew!' the Dean boomed. And then stopped and stared at me. 'And what do we have here?'

If I could've crawled into a knothole in the wood panelling and pulled it in after me, I would've. The Dean was big and blustery and white-haired, not a man to mess with. My face blazed red as the carpet, damp as Andrew's full lips after a sip of his coffee.

'This young man is Rufus Nerdlinger. He needs to see you, Dean. Apparently, quite urgently.'

'Well, OK, OK! I've got a few minutes before my first appointment,' the Dean bellowed, glancing at his watch. 'Come into my office, then.' He turned to Andrew. 'Bring my coffee in too, will you?'

Coffee. My loins shrivelled at the very word. Sunk deep between my legs when I trailed after the Dean into his office, and saw the vastness and seriousness of it all.

The man's office was lined with books and paintings and furnished with leather chairs and a huge walnut desk as old and distinguished as the college itself. Andrew brought in a cup in a saucer, set it down on the Dean's desk, as the man himself settled down into his high-backed, padded chair behind the desk. The coffee was black, and steaming.

Andrew was just about to leave the two of us alone, when the Dean suddenly raised a hand and yelled, 'Wait a minute, Andrew, you forgot my cream!'

I shrivelled another few inches.

'Sorry, my mistake. I'll get it for you.'

A phone rang in the outer office.

'Sit down, sit down!' Dean Skinner shouted at me.

'Can I see you for a moment, Dean?' Andrew suddenly interjected, sticking his head back into the open door.

The Dean thumped his big hands down on the desk and shoved himself upright, exited his office.

The phone call, the cup of coffee on the desk. It was all coming together.

I heard muffled voices outside as I slipped over to the Dean's desk, in behind, in front of his cup of coffee. I looked down at it, up at the open door. I picked up the cup and turned my back and pulled my cock out of my pants, started desperately stroking.

I wasn't thinking, just doing, the key to any half-cocked

stunt going off. Only this one required full cock, and I wasn't even close, nowhere near erection, let alone ejaculation. A door slammed. I frantically tugged on my prick, pulling nothing but a raging soft-on.

'What are you doing?'

I almost jumped out of my skin. My cock leapt right into the steaming hot coffee. 'Yow!' I howled.

Andrew rushed around the desk and stared at me holding the coffee cup in one hand and my cock in the other. I was suspended in time and motion, and soon academically, I feared.

But then a smile broke over Andrew's plush lips, and his eyes beamed warmly. He walked closer to me, took my cock out of my hand and bent down and kissed it. 'There, does that feel better?'

I gaped at the guy. Now, *now* my cock surged with blood – in Andrew's warm, soft palm. He pulled gently on it, making me shiver with disbelief and excitement.

'The Dean won't be back for a while,' he stated, relieving me of the coffee cup and setting it back down on the desk, never taking his other hand off my cock. He stroked me harder and longer, my body and dick flooding with dizzying heat.

He kissed me on the mouth, all soft and wet. I sighed, blissfully, from up on a fluffy cloud. Things had changed so suddenly, my emotions roller-coasting from stark fear and dread to luscious love and lust, Andrew fondling my cock and kissing my lips. He dropped down to his knees on the carpet, took the swollen tip of my prick into his mouth.

'Oh my, yes!' I moaned, shimmering with pleasure.

Andrew's dark lips enveloped my purple knob. He sucked gently, making me sway back and forth, his other hand gliding up and down my shaft.

Then his mouth was gliding down my shaft, his hand retreating before the awesome oral descent to come to rest on my fuzzy nut sack. He consumed my prick in a liquid heat even more wicked than the coffee, milking my balls with his agile fingers.

I sunk my shaking hands into his soft hair, urging him on, and he moved his head back and forth, sucking on my prick. The whole room spun before my dazzled eyes. I'd come to play a pledge prank, and here I was getting my cock played by a virtuoso.

Andrew dove his mouth down to his hand and back up again, wet-vaccing my prong. He did it over and over, stretching me out longer and harder still, drawing the semen out of the sack he was so erotically kneading.

'Sweet Jesus!' I cried. 'I'm gonna come!'

He pulled his liquorice lips back up my glistening pink cock, disgorging the gleaming pole in truly magnificent fashion. Then he picked the coffee cup up off the desk and pointed my pipe at the dark contents. 'Come in this,' he said. 'I just ate breakfast and there's nothing else handy.'

Practical, as well as sexual; the man was damn near perfect.

His hand flew up and down my over-engorged length, pumping me. I whimpered, shuddered. Orgasm tidal-waved through my spasming body, up from my balls and on through my shaft and out through my slit, Andrew's pull way too much to resist.

I bucked, blasting semen into the coffee. Andrew had a heck of a time keeping me down and on target, but he obviously had a master's degree, the way he mastered my dick. He didn't spill a drop, shooting my entire load into the cup, creaming the coffee but good.

'Your turn,' he said at the spluttering end, unhanding me and climbing to his feet.

I thought about the Dean, storming back in at any moment. I thought about … Then I saw Andrew's dong, as he pulled it out of his dress pants. And I thought about nothing more than loving that ebony appendage.

He was long and thick and black as coffee, a single

72

swollen vein running down the top of his shining nightstick. I dropped to my knees in awe and grasped his cock in my worshipping hands.

He grunted and jerked. I stroked with both hands, covering every black, velvety inch of his dick with my covetous palms. I fisted, pumping up from his balls to his cap, shunting slick foreskin back and forth.

I dropped one hand off and cupped his hanging balls, squeezed the heavy, dangling sack. He groaned and grabbed at my hair, thrusting his dong into my moving hand. I jacked his cock and juggled his balls, staring into the stunning darkness of his powerful loins.

'Suck me! Suck me!' he gasped.

I licked my lips and looked at his beefy, purple-black cap. Then I opened my mouth and popped the hood inside, mouthing his knob like he'd mouthed mine. He reacted the same way, moaning and sinking his fingernails into my scalp.

I sealed my lips tight to his hood and tugged, twisting his balls with my hand. His body bent and his mouth gaped, my own maw full of that chew-toy top of his cock. I had to have more, all if I could manage it. I opened my mouth and throat wide as they'd go and swallowed up his dong inch by gleaming, bloated inch.

I couldn't consume his entire snake, just more than enough for both of us. I kept him locked down and shivering like that for a while, then pulled my head back, pushed it forward, sucking on his pipe.

'Yes, that's it!' he hissed, pumping to meet my sucking.

He jerked my head to and fro, my mouth sliding up and down his incredible length. I gagged only a couple of times, filling up on his cock, filling his balls with seed with my sucking. I squeezed those balls, bringing them to full boil.

'Get the cup! Get the cup!'

I blinked my eyes open, tears streaking down my cheeks. I grabbed the coffee cup off the desk, and Andrew yanked his dong out of my mouth, leaving me achingly empty. I filled the void by grabbing on to his dripping cock and pumping hard and quick, aiming that mammoth hood at the brew I'd already seasoned with my own creamer.

Andrew jerked, and jetted, his cock going off with a spurt in my jacking hand. He splattered a rope of white-hot jizz into the coffee, another, and another, and another; his pressurized hose jumping in my hand. I had a heck of a time controlling it, Andrew losing all control.

Just as I pumped the last drop of cream out of his slit, the outer door suddenly opened and closed.

'Get up! Quick!' Andrew rasped, pulling his spent snake out of my hand and tucking it into his pants, gesturing at me with his free hand.

I jumped to my feet, jostling the heady brew in its cup.

'There was no emergency down in the women's dorm shower room, Andrew!' the Dean blustered, barrelling into his office. 'Someone must've got their wires crossed.'

He looked at me. 'Ah, my coffee! Properly creamed now, I see.'

He reached forward to take the cup from me. And I did the only thing I could think of to maintain my academic standing – I drank down the frothy beverage in three hearty gulps.

The Dean stared at me. Andrew grinned at me.

I found out the true nature of the prank – played on me – later that day, when I saw Dean Skinner's handsome secretary and frat brother Emilio making out like madmen behind the library building. They'd obviously been in cahoots on the whole thing, Andrew giving and getting a good blowjob while Emilio got a good laugh.

I wasn't too disappointed, though. Despite the fact my reckless actions counted for nothing in my quest to be fully pledged, hadn't the pair shown me what true fraternity between men was all about, Greek-style?

I Am Matilda Jenks
by Tabitha Rayne

I am Matilda Jenks.

I am unremarkable. I am of average height, average build. My eyes are a nondescript blue – they appear brown in some lights and even hazel in others. My hair is what used to be called "mousy", but I'm guessing even that has a fancy name now – perhaps "dusky suede". God forbid we are average. For me, though, being average is an advantage. A certain physical anonymity is just what I require. Yes, exactly what I need.

To be completely unmemorable. The ultimate disguise. Even my one distinguishing feature is manufactured; a tattoo of a black cat on the outer edge of my left hand, the tail snaking up and around my pinkie. If anyone were to pay me close attention, they could identify me from this one unusual addition. But they don't. I may even be talking about you …

I left school and worked in a hotel to fund my way through college. You know the kind – all fat business men in suits being important. The studying fell by the wayside but the uniform stayed and here I am talking to you with a tray in my hand.

Let me show you what I mean …

I balance the tray on my forearm and knock quietly on the door. Room 616.

'Room service,' I say brightly and take a breath.

'Come in.' A voice like all the others commands and I

push the handle. It clicks open and I gather the tray in both hands and push the door with my hip. I enter. A man, dark-haired and portly, sits at the coffee table by the window. He has on a suit but no shoes. The air is thick and rank.

'About time,' he says, never looking up from his Very Important Documents. 'I ordered that nearly 20 minutes ago.'

'I'm very sorry, sir,' I say while I stand holding his breakfast, waiting for a signal. He waves his hand dismissively and I place the tray on the bureau. I pick up the leather-bound tab book and hold it out to him with a pen. 'May I have your signature, sir?' He looks up briefly but doesn't take me in. It occurs to me that he might think I'm asking for his autograph. 'For the tab,' I add quickly.

He pauses as his swollen fingers grip the offered pen.

'I'm not sure if I will sign for it.' A snarl curls at the corner of his mouth.

'As sir wishes.' I bow my head slightly and start to back out of the room. 'Will sir require anything else?'

His focus is back on to his Very Important Work and he absently waves me away once more.

In the corridor I open the tab book. There is a speedily scrawled name but the gratuity is left blank. I smile and kick off my shoes. The signal for the end of my shift. Don't worry, dear reader. Mr Important, though he will have no idea, will be seeing me again very soon.

'Ms Spanks is very busy. You will have to wait.' I can hear Henry, my assistant, through my intercom. I keep it on while they're waiting and only allow them entry when they have earned it. Only those who plead and beg for my attentions will be allowed admittance into my secret haven. I look at myself in my full-length gilt-framed mirror. I, of course, am ready. I have seamed Cuban heel stockings and snappers. My waist is corseted in to a tiny 20 inches and my breasts spill over the top into a full-cupped satin bra. My outfit is encrusted in sparkling jet stones – including the banding of my seamers. I pull on my black lotus blossom kimono and fasten the thick obi to the back. I haven't decided yet if my gentlemen callers will deserve the sight of my attire this evening. My nails are scarlet to mach my lips and my hair is scraped into an impossibly tight French roll. It took an hour to manicure my nails and hands to perfection and I pull on my long stretch opera gloves to hide this effort. It's mine. For me. Only the very, very good will be allowed to see these perfect talons.

I sit on the bed and stretch out my feet to a perfect point. I flex my toes to inspect the work. Through the black nylon, my polished nails gleam wickedly. I pull on a pair of black ballet points and slowly wrap my ankles in the satin strapping. Of all the phases of my dressing, this is my favourite. I lift my leg high as I stroke the long ribbon, lacing it through my fingers and feeling the block press into my toes. I look in the mirror – I can never resist a peek at my raised leg, and hold the ribbons like reins while I roll out my hips to see the black satin of my panties between my thighs. I love to tease myself like this. I love to know that while they wait, I can pleasure myself and not let them have any of it. I flex and point, flex and point. My legs are strong and lean and this self-scrutiny makes me want. I let the satin slide through my hands until only the very tip is left in my finger and thumbs. I have calculated this to perfection. At full stretch, I can pull my ballet slippers tight and hook my pinkie into the fabric of my panties. If I stretch really hard, I can feel the moistening folds of my pussy and my finger can slip in just a little. I love this. I love the way I can watch as my cheeks redden and my breasts swell.

'Please.' The intercom breaks my spell. 'When can I see her?' The voice is pleading but not enough.

'I'm sorry sir, but Ms Spanks is a very busy lady, as I'm sure you'll understand.' Henry has done the trick.

Sometimes I'll let my fingers trail and explore, sinking

them deep into my pussy and fucking myself while they plead for me next door. Then I'll send them on their way. Sometimes, I think that's all they want. It's strange, but I think I can tell.

My pussy is twitching but I snatch my fingers away and finish tying the bows at my ankles.

I am no longer Little Miss Unremarkable, Matilda Jenks. By night, I am the extremely memorable Ms Tilly Spanks.

'Henry -' I use my strict tone and press the intercom with the tip of my fingernail '- please come through.'

'Yes, miss,' he says, then I imagine him turning to the waiting man. 'She doesn't sound very happy, sir. Is there something you need to tell me?' I visualise the man shrinking a little into his seat and trembling inwardly. They are always so fearful of offending me, so worried I'll reject them and send them on their way. Henry knocks gently so the man doesn't catch wind of the code. Soft, soft, then slide of the knuckles, then one more soft. It's so subtle, and Henry does it exactly the same way every time.

'Enter,' I say while releasing the lock. Henry is beaming and trying not to giggle. I check that the intercom is still on.

'Henry, I have some concerns and I would like you to keep this in the strictest of confidence.' We both sidle glances to the speaker and strain to hear the shuffling of the client leaning in.

'Oh yes, Ms Spanks, you know you can rely on me for the utmost discretion.'

He grins and looks me up and down lasciviously and mouths, 'Show me your tit.' I obey and slide the kimono open to reveal my nipple resting over the balcony bra. He licks his lips and nods back at the intercom.

'It's just I think there may be some counterfeit invitations going round.'

'Ms Spanks, no!' Henry declares so dramatically, I could almost forget he's in on this.

'Could you show me the invite the gentleman outside

gave you?'

'Yes, though it seems to be in order.' He reaches deep into his trouser pocket, pulling the fabric taut over his package. I feel my pussy begin to melt at the stirring in his pants and I slide my heels apart and pull the kimono to the side. Henry throws the little gold note on to the table, the same one I quietly dropped on Mr Important's room service tray this very afternoon. He had been quick to take up the offer of a night with the hotel's more secret services. Henry can obviously see my want rising in the flush of my cheeks and lunges at me, one hand around the back of my neck, pulling me into a ferocious kiss, and the other diving straight between my legs. He knows me so well. My pussy is clenching and unclenching as he dips only his fingertips into the moistening entrance. It is at first a delicate probing, mirroring the trail of tiny kisses he is placing over my mouth. Every now and then his tongue darts between my lips to meet mine and his finger does the same in my pussy. I lean into him, daring him to kiss me harder, fuck me deeper with his fingers. I tip my pelvis towards him and he maddeningly pulls away. He nudges my attention back to the intercom. I am panting now, and frustrated.

'No, Henry,' I say while he takes his middle finger and licks the length of it, sliding it into his succulent lips. 'This is very bad, I'm afraid. This gentleman seems to be in possession of the contraband I told you about.'

'What?' Henry raises the glistening finger to my face. 'The invite is a fake?' he says incredulously, then reaches down to my panties. I tremble as he pulls them to the side and slides his finger full length into my hungry pussy. I gasp and hear a shuffling on the intercom and some breaths. I rock on to his solid digit, hooking into that perfect spot deep inside. I am slumping on to him now and it feels like he is taking my full weight on that finger. He starts humping my clit with the heel of his hand and I whimper and pant, clawing at his crotch, trying to find the zipper.

'Henry, this is strictly against protocol,' I cry as I pull his gleaming shaft from his pants. 'What if someone were to hear us?' The panting in the intercom becomes a growl and I am so wet to know every sexual noise we make is being listened to.

'Who can hear us?' Henry grabs me by the hair at my neck and spins me round over the bed, pushing me on to it. He pulls my satin panties down under my garters just enough to reveal my arse. He smoothes the skin slowly with the palm of his hand, trailing his fingers into the crease between the mounds. Then, *thwack,* he spanks me hard. The sting is ferocious but I sway back, arching my rear high for more. *Thwack*; again I wince but blood races to my pussy. I hear heavy breathing on the intercom.

'Henry!' I shriek as his hand comes down hard a third time. My thighs are moist with my juices and my legs are trembling. Henry has the tip of his cock flirting with my entrance. I clench and unclench, pushing back, trying to catch it. He is a master of the tease. He slides his thumb into me easily and twists it about, coating it with my want. He spreads my arse cheeks apart with his palms and fingers and slides the glistening thumb out of my pussy and up, gently probing me. I tighten up and he slowly winds me open, just a little, before removing his hands and giving me one hell of a smack. My cheeks are throbbing and stinging and I cry out with pain and desire.

'Just fuck me, Henry!' I reach up and pull my bra down to let my breasts spill out and sway over the bed linen. I lean in a little to let the fabric graze my nipples and at last feel the pressure of Henry's dick at my opening. The sounds on the intercom are heated and I imagine Mr Important with his cock in his hand, stark against the dark pinstripe suit, and I yelp with the excitement of knowing he is as hard as Henry. I imagine what it would be like to have both of them enter me at the same time. The thought floods me with desire and suddenly Henry forces his dick right into me and I swallow him up. He pulls out and thrusts again even harder and slaps me on the arse once more.

'Oh God, Henry, harder, harder,' I say as he fucks me deeper and spanks me. I open my legs wide and reach to my clit as his thumb takes its place at my arse. I am being thoroughly worked on and my want builds until I am writhing in the sheets in sweet agony of pleasure.

'Open the peephole,' I command and Henry withdraws his beautiful cock and reaches over to a small hatch in the door. There is a shuffling from the speaker, then the intercom falls silent as Mr Important takes his place at the door. I roll on to my back. Knowing exactly where the best view is I position myself on the bed and stretch my legs up and open to show off my soaking panties to our voyeur.

'Lick me, Henry,' I purr and he falls to his knees before me, tugging my underwear to the side and diving his face into the folds of my sex. I let my head fall back as he laps at my clit, pulling hard at the fabric, using it to press into the flesh of my buttocks. With his other hand, he shoves two rigid fingers deep into my throbbing pussy. I twitch upwards on to them, undulating my pelvis, fucking his mouth. His tongue is strong on my tiny peak and I feel my pleasure welling in the pit of my womb. It begins to rise and I cry out and grab Henry by the hair and wrap my legs around his head as I come over his face with his fingers rammed deep inside me. He keeps the fingers still but flicks his tongue gently over my clit to keep my orgasm coming.

'Stop, stop!' I pant. 'Stop, I can't take any more!' But my legs keep him firmly clamped in place until my twitching subsides and his own desire takes over.

'Turn over,' he commands again and I obey, excited by the thought of the invasion. I just make it on to my front when his thick rod thrusts straight into me hard, fast, and furious, just the way I like it. He slams into me again and again until my pussy is raw. At last, I feel the unmistakable stuttering of his movements and, with a jerk and a groan, he comes deep inside me, gripping my hips hard. He flops on top of me and we lie still for a minute or two, basking in the relief of a hard and fast fuck. Eventually, I roll him off me and slide out underneath to the door. I smile slowly as I flip the peep hole shut.

I balance the tray on my forearm and knock quietly on the door. Room 616.

'Room service,' I say brightly and take a breath.

'Enter.' I push the handle. It clicks open and I gather the tray in both hands and push the door with my hip. Mr Important sits at the coffee table by the window. 'About time,' he says, never looking up from his Very Important Documents. 'I ordered that nearly 20 minutes ago.'

'I'm very sorry, sir,' I say while I stand holding his breakfast, waiting for a signal. He waves his hand dismissively and I place it on the bureau. I pick up the leather-bound tab book and hold it out to him with a pen. 'May I have your signature, sir?' He looks up briefly but doesn't take me in. 'For the tab,' I add quickly.

He pauses as his swollen fingers grip the offered pen. Is that a flicker of recognition?

'I'm not sure if I will sign for it.' A snarl curls at the corner of his mouth.

'As sir wishes,' I say, bowing my head slightly and begin to back out of the room. 'Will sir require anything else?'

'Actually, yes,' he says and hands me a little envelope. 'See this gets to room 822.'

'Of course, sir.' I close the door carefully behind me and open the envelope. It contains a note on hotel paper and five £50 notes.

Ms Spanks, a little something extra. Treat yourself.

I drop the note in a nearby bin and pocket the cash.

I smile and kick off my shoes.

Discretion Required
by Heidi Champa

I glanced at the clock, as I navigated the winding streets of the palatial community. The directions sat on the passenger's seat beside me, leading me deeper into the unknown part of town. I'd only ever driven into Woodlawn Hills twice, to admire the majestic houses from the comfort of my car. Never in my wildest dreams did I ever think I'd be inside one of the mansions everyone in town coveted.

When I made the last turn indicated on my directions, I was greeted by wrought iron gates, which kept prying eyes from really seeing much of the house. According to your instructions, I was to press the button on the call box and wait. So I did what you told me to do, my hand shaking slightly as I reached out of my window to press the red button on the slate-grey box that was situated on the left side of the driveway. I waited, sweat forming on my palms as the seconds turned into minutes. Finally, the iron gates started to move, and once the opening was large enough, I pulled my car inside the wall border of the house.

My mouth fell open as I took in the sheer expansiveness of the castle-style home that stood before me. I pulled my car into the area you specified in the email, careful to follow your directives to the letter. The last thing I wanted to do was upset you. It wasn't just because I needed the money. I also truly needed to do what you told me to do. I could have earned spare cash in any number of ways. This opportunity was about more than just cash. It was about a secret, powerful need I had never been brave enough to satisfy. Before now. Before you.

I exited the car, my eyes fixed on the enormous double doors I was approaching. Your email told me not to knock, just to turn the knob and walk right in. It felt wrong, as if I were some kind of thief or something. But, I did as you instructed and entered the most palatial foyer I'd ever seen outside a movie theatre. The ornate staircase was in front of me and split into two directions about halfway up. You wanted me to go left at the fork and go to the fifth door on the right. Even though the house was seemingly empty, I felt your eyes on me. Part of the deal is that you would have your eyes on me at all times. My cunt moistened as I moved up each step, clenching as I approached my destination, knowing your gaze was following my every move. My heels clicked on the marble floors, the only sound in the house.

The fifth door was heavy mahogany and when I pushed it open, it led into a bedroom that looked like it had never been used, completely untouched, each detail perfect. The bed was enormous; a black bag sat near the headboard. You had put it there for me and it contained each implement you would want me to use, for your pleasure. I walked towards the bed and that's when I saw the small piece of paper lying on the pristine duvet. Your handwriting was exquisite; the thick card stock felt more like fabric than actual paper.

Your note told me to take a shower and to enjoy myself. I was to be wet and ready when I returned to the bedroom, but I was to save the real show for later. You just wanted to see me soapy under the water. The marble-covered bathroom was just off the bedroom, and was bigger than my whole apartment. The lights were soft and the shower was big enough for a whole group of people to get inside. I undressed, tossing my clothes aside, and tried to sneak a peek around the room, to see if I could spot any cameras. I knew they were there, but as much as I searched, I could see no evidence of their existence. You were too smart to give your secrets away like that.

When we first started corresponding on the Internet, you watching me through a webcam as I broadcast from my own bedroom, I never thought I'd end up naked in your shower, ready to give you the live version of a performance I'd been giving you for months in cyberspace. I was desperate to please you and you knew it. Each time we logged in together, you upped the ante until you had me just where you wanted me. I should have been nervous, but I wasn't. My desire had drowned every other feeling out, leaving only the need behind. Which was exactly what you wanted.

I turned on the water, which sprayed from four chrome showerheads, stepping inside before it had turned warm. Once it did, the steam started to rise in the cool room, and I hoped your view wasn't too obscured by the fog. I took my time soaping up and tried to clear my mind of everything but what was to come. My nipples strained every time my hands got near them, and it was difficult not to roll them between my soap-covered fingers. I resisted the temptation to provide myself with some quick relief, to reach down and stroke my swollen clit to relieve some of the tension welling up inside me. I knew it would upset you. That was the last thing I wanted to do.

Once I was dry, I walked naked into the bedroom and stood at the foot of the bed, the cool air raising goosebumps on my skin. My eyes scanned over the whole room, my arms stiff at my sides. When I heard you speak, I nearly jumped out of my skin. Your voice was crisp and clear, deep and powerful, but I had no idea where it was coming from.

'Turn around, please. Let me see your face.'

I swivelled around, my eyes still searching for where the camera might be hidden. Again, your voice filled the room, making me jump.

'You can keep looking if you like, but you won't find the cameras. I made sure of that. I told you, I like discretion. So now, what should I call you?'

I cleared my throat, just to make sure I could still make a sound.

'Joan. My name is Joan. Sir.'

It wasn't, but for some reason I didn't want to give you my real name. It only seemed fair, as I didn't know your name either. It really didn't matter what you called me. I wasn't there to get to know you. I was there so you could use my pleasure for your own. My cunt was aching, just waiting for your first instructions.

'OK, Joan. Grab that bag that's sitting on the bed. Then come back and stand right where you are now.'

I walked around the bed, the soft material of the duvet rubbing against my bare leg. I could almost feel the weight of your gaze as I grabbed the small black leather bag and moved back to my first position. My footprints were still visible in the thick pile of the carpet. I heard the crackle of your microphone before you started speaking.

'Good, now why don't you go ahead and sit on the bed and open the bag, Joan. See what I have for you today. I think you'll like it.'

My hands shook as I pulled the zipper open and spread the sides of the bag open. Inside, the first thing I saw was a huge bottle of lube. As I continued to look, I came across dildos and plugs of various shapes and sizes and a small towel folded neatly underneath it all. I looked up, at nothing in particular, waiting for you to say something else.

'Take it all out and set it on the bed, Joan. Lay it out nice and neat. I want you to have everything at your disposal. The last thing I want is for you to be fumbling around.'

I did as you said and laid everything out on the bed, the toys lined up from smallest to largest. The towel and the lube sat next to them and I crouched down to put the bag on the floor. Before I could stand back up all the way, I heard your voice.

'Good girl, Joan. Now get on all fours, on the bed. Point that wet pussy the same way you were facing before. Put it up nice and high, just like you've done for me before.'

I crawled onto the bed and put my elbows down onto the mattress. My ass lifted as I lowered my head to the bed, my cheeks spread open as I tried to control my breathing. My pussy was hot and desperate for attention. I wondered if it was wet enough for you to see it. It certainly felt like it.

'Good, now reach back and touch yourself. Play a little bit. Show me how soaking wet you are, Joan.'

I let my finger slid inside my pussy, groaning at the intrusion. It slid in so easily, I couldn't resist adding a second finger. I pumped in and out, my cunt so wet every movement was audible. I hoped you could hear it. Just as I was about to rub my thumb over my clit, your voice rang out again.

'That's nice, Joan. Now, I want you to lie down and pick up the blue dildo. Start working it into your pussy. I want to see you take it all. I know you can do it.'

I did as you said and eased onto my back, making sure my pussy was still on full display for you. I eyed the blue dildo, just a little bit bigger and thicker than what I was used to. Undeterred, I pressed the blunted tip of the dildo to my centre and slid it inside my pussy. I started to open up as I pumped the fake cock inside me, wishing it were yours. I didn't censor my reactions, every gasp and groan the real thing. As I pushed the dildo deeper still, I heard your voice again.

'Play with your nipples, Joan. Just like you did in the shower.'

I stopped moving the dildo, just for a moment as I moved my hand up my chest. I let out a deep breath and rolled my tightened nipple between my thumb and finger. After both my nipples were rock hard, I started fucking myself again, enjoying the full feeling for a long moment on each stroke before I pulled the silicon cock part of the way out again. I fucked myself slowly, getting used to being filled, the ridged and bumped surface hitting all the right spots. Your voice was there, ready to urge me on.

'That's it, Joan. Fuck that sweet little pussy. Just like that. A little faster now. Really work it in there. Let me see how you like to be fucked.'

Your voice echoed off the walls as I thrust the dildo in my cunt as far as it would go. My cunt gripped and stretched around it, my clit begging for some attention. From you. Finally, you gave it.

'Good girl, Joan. Now, give that clit a rub. Nice and slow. But, remember the rules. No coming until I say. So be careful.'

I whimpered as I touched myself, my clit sliding beneath my thumb to the same rhythm I used to fuck my own pussy. My hips rocked back and forth, the dual stimulation almost too much to bear. I heeded your warning and slowed down a bit, trying to stave off the inevitable. The cock in my pussy felt so good, I wished again it was yours. Someday, I hoped you'd give me the honour of fucking me for real. For now, this would have to do.

'Go nice and slow, Joan. I want you fucking that cunt deep and hard. You look so fucking hot. Do you like it, Joan?'

I opened my eyes, trying to find the ability to speak.

'Oh, God. Yes, sir. I love it.'

'Good. Now, give yourself two more good thrusts and take that dildo out of your pussy.'

I relished the last two strokes of the dildo and did as you said. Everything stopped for a moment as I stared into space, waiting for you.

'Now, use the red one. I want that big, fat cock all the way up your tight little cunt, do you hear me, Joan? I want to see you stretched to your limit. Use the lube if you need to.'

As I began to lube the fake, red cock, I marvelled at its girth. I knew it would be tough, but I would have done anything to please you. I stretched out on my back and I started working the cock into my pussy, the first few inches going smoother than I thought they would. As I pushed on, the first pangs of pain started. I tried again, but to no avail. I sighed, hoping the deep breathing would help, but the dildo remained where it was. Until I heard your voice, stern and rough.

'Keep going, Joan. You will take more of that cock. I want it buried deep inside you. Don't disappoint me now. You want to keep coming back here, don't you?'

'Yes, sir. Yes, I do.'

'Then take it. Take it all for me.'

I bore down on the unyielding dildo, emboldened by your words. After a few seconds of agony, the cock moving in and out of me started to feel amazing. I gasped for air, the pain mixing with pleasure so sublime, I could have cried.

'Good girl. Now fuck that pussy. Nice and slow like before.'

I did as you asked, barely able to stand the sensation. I made small circles over my clit, the edge getting dangerously close. But I forced myself to hold off, knowing how upset you would be if I disobeyed you. I started to get used to the massive red dildo, enjoying every inch of it. I fucked myself with abandon, sweat forming on my forehead. I was writhing on the bed, unable to control how my body was moving. I started to fuck my cunt as fast and as rough as I could manage, under the circumstances. I growled through gritted teeth each time I pushed the cock all the way inside.

'You're ready to come, aren't you, Joan?'

'Yes, sir. I am. Please, let me come.'

You laughed, the sound hollow as I continued my self-torture.

'I'm not quite done with you yet, Joan. Take the dildo out. Right now.'

I grumbled as I did what you asked, the red dildo leaving me empty and hungry for more. I rubbed my clit furiously, but it just wasn't the same.

'Now, be a good girl and put that black plug up your ass. It isn't too big, so it shouldn't be a problem for you. And I know you like it in the ass, Joan. You told me yourself.'

I was so crazed with lust, I dove on the butt plug, lubing it and working it inside me inch by inch. Trying to relax wasn't easy, as worked up as I was, but I needed to come. The plug teased me, my cunt getting wetter with each passing moment. Finally, I nestled the flared base in between my cheeks and looked up at the walls expectantly, trying to imagine you with your cock in your hand somewhere in the house. But you could have been anywhere.

'Gorgeous, Joan. You have a spectacular ass. Now roll onto your back and play with your nipples again. Keep those thighs spread so I can see you.'

'Please, sir. I don't think I can take much more.'

'You can and you will. Now do what you're told.'

I twisted and pinched my nipples, the same way I had into my webcam all those months ago. It felt good, but it wasn't enough to get me off. You knew it. Another laugh came through the sound system as I squirmed around on the bed, my toes curling as I went back and forth between agony and ecstasy. My ass clenched around the butt plug and I rolled my head from side to side, trying to get myself under control.

'You want to come so bad, don't you, Joan?'

'Yes, sir. Please. Please, I want to come for you. Please, let me come. I'll do anything you want.'

'I know you will, Joan. Now, pick up that blue dildo again and fuck yourself. Be a good girl and go slow. I can't wait to watch you come.'

The last words were barely out of your mouth before I had the fake cock in hand and slid it back inside me. I was stuffed full and it felt better than I ever imagined it would. I didn't ask for permission to touch my clit, but you didn't object when I did. It was torture to move so slow, but I did as I was told. My body was like a tightened coil and with each pass of my fingers over my hard nub, the orgasm I'd been craving got ever closer. The rumble of your voice was just enough to push me over the elusive edge, hitting my ears just as the blue dildo was in me to the hilt.

'Come, you little slut. Come for me now.'

Once again, I was obedient and did as you asked. I nearly screamed as my whole body wracked with pleasure. I could no longer control the movements of my body, my hips and hands moving without conscious thought. Just when I thought the first wave was over, a second wave of ecstasy crashed over me and knocked me flat. I kept rubbing my clit and fucking my pussy until I could no longer breathe. I was spent, my whole body limp. When I could finally move, I took the plug out of my ass and set everything back on the towel you provided me. The room was silent as I collapsed back on the bed and stared at the ceiling as I tried to catch my breath. I could barely sit up, I felt weak, but I knew I should get going. I got to my feet and looked around the room, unsure of what to do next. Luckily, your voice cut through all the confusion.

'That was lovely, Joan. Don't worry about anything. I'll clean up. Should we say the same time next week?'

'Yes, sir. I'd like that.'

'I'll be in touch, Joan.'

I went to the bathroom to clean up and got dressed as quickly as I could. After splashing some cold water on my face, I made my way downstairs. There was an envelope sitting on a small table by the door, thicker than I thought it would be. I picked it up right before I walked out the door. My car had a bit of trouble starting, but soon enough, I got it going again.

As I took one last look at the place, I saw you, framed in an upstairs window. I couldn't see your face, just your hand pressed against the glass. You watched me as I left, until I pulled on to the street and back to my real life.

Airtight
by Dominic Santi

Panama Jack is an asshole. Not that executive officers of Navy nuclear submarines are known for their warm, fuzzy personalities. But Panama Jack takes being an asshole to new heights – or depths, as the case often is when we're underway. When we're in the yard for repairs, he's even worse. He walks like he's got a stick up his ass, his hair cut to perfect regulation length as he struts along the pier like he expects even the fucking flagpole to salute him.

Panama Jack's wife is young and pretty, with long, curly blonde hair and baby blue eyes that can make your cock spring to attention with just one wink. She wears short, hot pink skirts with matching stiletto heels and no panties. Her blouses are cut damn near to her navel and hug the biggest, creamiest natural tits I'd ever seen. The nipples are the size of the bottom of a beer can, with tips that stand out dark and stiff because she begs to have them sucked when she's being fucked.

Normally, a mere petty officer would not know the particulars of the sex life of his XO's wife. However, most XOs aren't stupid enough to volunteer for extra duty on their fucking anniversary. Amanda had just finished her first strawberry marguerita when she sashayed over to our table and asked who wanted to fuck.

I was the only one who recognised her. The other five guys, all enlisted, like me, had joined the crew since last year's Submariners Ball. Not that they would have noticed once her next marguerita arrived. She rolled the frosty glass over her nipple, giggling when it poked out into her silky blue top.

'Ooh! My titty's cold! Who wants to warm it up with a big, slurpy anniversary kiss?'

Five faces damn near knocked each other silly in the rush to be first in line. I paid for her drink, giving the waitress an extra $20 to go away and ignore us. The look Amanda gave me told me two things: she wasn't drunk, and she remembered who'd paid for her drinks at the Ball as well. She quirked an eyebrow at me and smiled.

'There's just one itty bitty catch to us having a real fun party.'

Five sets of eyes froze, riveted to her face – Jensen's looking up since he wasn't willing to take his lips off the prize he'd won by sheer brute force. Amanda ran a finger down her neckline, tracing Jensen's jaw before trailing slowly back up. He shivered, sucking harder to keep from losing his grip. Amanda shuddered and smiled.

'My husband's in the Navy, and he's not on shore right now,' she said in her honeyed Southern drawl. 'He likes to watch.' She plucked a cell phone from her teeny tiny purse and held it out to me. 'If you'll take the pictures, I'll lead the parade – startin' with a big ol' strip tease, as soon as we get to my hotel room.'

Her husband wasn't on shore because he was in his office on the barge next to the pier where our boat was tied up – about two miles away. But unless he called in another command officer to relieve him, which would mean explaining why he'd dragged them out of bed on one of their only nights home before we really did go back out to sea again, there wasn't much chance ol' Panama Jack could do anything other than watch and fume and maybe beat off. Hell, who knew – maybe he did like to watch. I was willing to take his wife's word for it. Jack's an asshole. I was horny. His wife was fucking hot. Payback's a bitch, ya know?

The other guys didn't know who our "date" was. In fact, since Jack had left the Ball as soon as he could, I doubted he knew I'd met his hot wife either. I took the phone and followed the other guys outside to a cab, reassuring Jensen that while he had to let go of the lady's tit for the duration of the ride, he could suck it again while we rode her hard and wet later on.

The hotel room was classy, a result, no doubt, of the XO's wife's flashing the platinum-plus credit card Jack was so fond of drawing slowly out of his pocket when the correct social occasion required. Jack was fond of drama. Obviously, so was his wife. As to which part of watching his wife fuck other men turned him on – not my fucking problem. Amanda had pre-programmed Panama Jack's cell phone number into her speed dial. I sat down in the comfy armchair on the far side of the room, unbuttoned my fly, and pulled out my dick. Then I pointed the camera at the orgy starting on the bed and clicked the first time.

Hot Wife

I figured a good text message would keep each photo in the proper perspective. And Amanda was hot. She was kneeling in the middle of the bed, her top pulled open to reveal her obviously well-sucked nipple. I hit SEND. In case the viewer might miss that little detail, Amanda was fingering the still-wet tip, pursing her lips to air kiss the camera. I zeroed in, took a close-up, added the title *Hot Nipple* and hit SEND again.

5 Horny Sailors from the Bar

Since Amanda had protected the others by not introducing herself to them, I figured ol' Jack needed a reminder that while this shindig was part of his relationship with his wife, everybody else was just along for the ride. They had no idea who she was – other than a pretty, horny woman they'd picked up in the bar. As Jensen once more latched onto his prize, I hit SEND again.

Sucking a Tasty Tit

From the way Jensen's cheeks were moving, he was in hog heaven. Amanda closed her eyes and held him to her breast, her lips parting as he sucked harder. I clicked just as she shuddered.

Good Tit Work, Good Come

Oh yeah. That blush showed she'd definitely climaxed. I hit SEND – twice.

As the flush faded, Amanda rose slowly to her feet. Over the next few minutes, I got pictures of Amanda doing a slow, seductive strip tease for her mesmerized audience. I caught Brown and Garcia beating off as she unhooked her bra, letting it fall the rest of the way off as her huge, creamy breasts fell free. I got shot after shot of Davis and Chen with their hands wrapped around their dicks, their eyes glued to the awesome sight of Amanda shimmying out of that skin-tight hot pink skirt and peeling off her lacy white panties. SEND SEND SEND SEND

I deleted the cache and started all over again. Amanda had a gross of rubbers on the bed, along with the biggest bottle of lube I'd seen outside a sex toy store on the Pacific Rim.

Jensen kept zeroing back in on her breasts. The others had progressed further south. From the looks on their faces, there was no such thing as sloppy seconds. I caught each of them, face down and sweaty as they balanced on their hands and fucked her one after the other in the military-appropriate missionary position

Snapper

No Sloppy Seconds

Appreciating Good Pussy

Fucking Good Pussy

SEND SEND SEND SEND

Sailors Have Big Cocks

I'd seen the XO in the shower, so I knew that wasn't universally true. But I figured it would piss him off to know that while he was hunched over his instruments, someone –

several someones – with bigger instruments than he had were fucking his wife's brains out, in a hotel room he was paying for.

Fucking and Sucking

Even Jensen joined in. Amanda went nuts, throwing her head back and screaming as he sucked so hard with each thrust that her nipple pulled up like she was suspended by it. When Amanda starting coming, kicking her legs and bucking up as her skin flushed, I took a second full-face picture of Jensen's cheeks sucked hollow as he ground against her.

Talent

SEND SEND SEND

From the way Amanda was howling, it had been a while since she'd had a come that good. I shook my head. Jack had been in port for a week, and his wife was still in need. That was just wrong. So I took another picture.

Neglected Wife Gets Relief

Let ol' Jack fucking stew on that one for a while!

SEND

The other five each got their cocks sucked and did her doggy-style up the ass, going through a whole slew of rubbers each time the group rotated like kids at a party playing musical chairs.

SEND SEND SEND SEND SEND SEND

After a while, I dispensed with the text titles, smiling at the monologue running through my head as I raised and lowered my arm, looking for the perfect angles.

That's for the extra day of duty.

Garcia and Brown had rolled her on her side, donning fresh rubbers and lubing themselves up as they positioned themselves. The look of greedy hunger on Amanda's face as Garcia slid into her pussy was worth a whole series of pictures. Her wide-eyed, gape-mouthed astonishment when Brown slowly worked his huge dong up her ass was worth even more, but I was too busy beating off to get every nuance. Fuck, that woman was hot! Fucking fuck! A woman like that was wasted on a tightwad jerk like Panama Jack! I settled for highlights, my mind racing as I showed why the walls were ringing with her shrieks.

That's for making me do mess crank duty for an extra week.

Amanda's eyes were huge as Brown bottomed out and ground against her.

This is for the 0600 field day chores!

I aimed the camera directly at her crotch, catching a perfect shot of both Garcia and Brown buried balls deep, their asses tight as they stretched her pussy so wide she opened her mouth when she screamed.

And this one – oh yeah, make her make that face again! This time I aimed the camera full at her face, catching the way her eyes rolled back as she came again. *That's for disapproving my leave chit, you asshole!*

SEND SEND SEND

Things were getting crowded on the bed as Davis straddled her face. He grinned like a fool as she licked his shaved, low-hanging balls. It took Jensen a while to work his way in above Garcia, but our resident tit-sucker was determined to get his prize. Then Chen was standing on the bed over the lot of them, his fist flying over his dick as his body tensed to come. I hit video just in time to catch Amanda's squeal being muffled as Davis's cock slid down her throat.

The sound made Chen come. As Chen's semen gorped like rain onto Amanda's tits, Jensen shot into the bed. Amanda shrieked again, the sound rising and falling as Davis fucked her mouth, then roared out his climax. I raised the camera as Amanda bucked up again, her body tensing and flushing, clear juice squirting from her pussy as Brown came up her ass and Garcia filled the rubber in her pussy with his cock juice.

Airtight!

I thought the words, but I was beating my own dick too hard and fast to type. Watching Amanda come by making five men shoot their wads was the hottest fucking thing I'd ever seen! Davis groaned loudly and fell to the side, his softening cock thick and heavy against her lips. Garcia and Brown were holding her tight, laughing and telling her she was one damn fine woman.

Jensen had already climaxed, but he was still sucking her tit. Worshipping it. Making her face flush as she once again looked me right in the eye. She was going to come again. Hard. Real hard.

'Do it!' she pleaded, her fingers flying over her clit as Brown's and Garcia's cocks fell free. Her asshole gaped and her pussy lips were swollen as she once more took Davis's almost-soft cock between her lips. Then Brown and Garcia and Davis had their fingers back inside her, fucking her with their hands as Jensen sucked one nipple and Chen worked the other with his finger. I raised the camera, and as Amanda screamed again, I clicked – and came.

A long time later, I sent the rest of the pictures, including the video with the simple subject line of *Airtight*. I hoped the XO was sitting in his office with his dick in his hand, waiting to come while the rest of us lounged naked on the bed eating room service pizza and drinking expensive wine on his dime. His wife was a great fuck and a hot woman. My buddies and I were always going to be glad to oblige her. I hoped Panama Jack really did like watching, because he was going to be getting a lot of photos whenever I was in port.

SEND

Perks of the Job
by Kay Jaybee

Rachel shook slightly as she sent the text. *Do I have the correct number? Is that you, sir?*

She cupped her hands around her mug of tea as she sat in the cheap and cheerful café, her gaze fixed on her phone – waiting with a stomach full of uncertainty for a reply.

Rachel nearly slopped its contents all over the plastic tablecloth as her mobile began to ring. She snapped her phone to her ear quickly, her heart thudding so hard she could feel its beat in the pulse of her neck. She hadn't expected a call. She had been sure that Ryan would stick to the more anonymous medium of the text message.

'Yes, you do have the right number. Are you in the café as arranged?'

'Yes.'

'Right, this is what is going to happen.' His voice was a lot rougher than she'd ever heard it before. But then, Rachel thought as she pushed the phone closer to her ear, afraid that the few other café dwellers might accidentally overhear what she was about to be told, he hasn't been turned on when we've talked before. She knew he was now – everything about Ryan's tone spoke of a man with a hard-on. 'Is the regular waitress there? The student one with the tits that are fighting to break out of her shirt, and the tight black cardigan that should make her look like an old maid, but actually makes her look like a hooker?'

Rachel lowered her voice further, worried the girl in

question would hear her, 'If you mean the one with brown hair and blonde streaks, then yes.'

'I want you to stay sat *exactly* where you are. Fix your eyes on her. Picture her behind the counter. I am standing in front of her. You are behind her. I want you to imagine her on all fours. My cock is in her mouth. I want to watch your face as she brings me off. How does it feel? Tell me now. How would seeing that make you feel?'

Colour infused Rachel's face. As she watched the waitress move around behind the counter, sorting out glasses and bottles of cola, Rachel tried not to make her observation of the younger girl's movements obvious.

Even though Ryan wasn't there, Rachel felt as though his eyes were unwaveringly on her. There was something about him - she knew her boss was dangerous, she knew he was taking advantage of the fact that she needed to earn some extra cash, and yet that seemed to arouse her rather than annoy her.

It didn't take much effort for Rachel to visualise the waitress on her hands and knees, her short black skirt hooked up over her hips and backside, her thong in tatters on the floor, and her tights ripped in the haste of their removal. Ryan had his combats at his ankles, his boxers yanked to one side to allow his solid erection room to manoeuvre towards the lapping and sucking mouth of the café girl.

'Talk to me, dirty girl. Tell me right now, I don't have much time.' Ryan's voice seemed to be coming from further and further away as Rachel began to see the image he'd created for her with growing clarity. 'Tell me, bitch, how does it feel?'

'Can't I text you instead?'

'No.'

Conscious of being overheard, Rachel murmured, 'But someone might hear me!'

'We had a deal.'

Rachel swallowed. They did have a deal.

Speaking so she was only just audible, picking up the grease-spotted menu that had been languishing before her, using it to hide her mouth from those on the neighbouring tables, she began, 'My tits are so hard. I can see everything as though it was really happening - I really can. You're pounding into her; I can feel her arse pushing back against my legs with each thrust you make. Her body is rocking, but she doesn't want to stop, and I know from the eager noises coming from the corners of her mouth that, despite her messed-up state, she's loving it.'

'Are you wet? Right now - as you sit there, are your knickers sticking to your nasty little snatch?'

Caught up in the hungry pace of his voice, Rachel nodded as well as spoke, almost forgetting this was a conversation over the phone and not in person. She had to remind herself that she couldn't really feel the touch of his rough hands against her chest, as much as she longed to. 'I am. My jeans are beginning to get damp. My liquid isn't being held by my panties alone.' She took a deep breath, and carried on her narration. 'I have my gaze hooked into yours as the waitress milks you off. You don't say anything, but I know what you want me to do, and so I bend a little, smacking the rounded flesh of her arse with the flat of my hand.'

The voluble gasp from the other end of the phone told Rachel that she had judged her caller's fantasy correctly. 'As I spank her, she shifts forwards, her throat taking your dick in deeper. As you push your hips harder, she gags a little, and her butt comes back to my waiting hand, which strikes her once more, leaving a pleasing pink patch of flesh in its wake.'

'Then what will you do?' He didn't have to tell Rachel that he was wanking; she could tell. She sped up her erotic scenario, unsure how she was going to prevent herself from coming in sympathy with him, and thus giving the café customers   more   in-house   entertainment   than   that establishment had seen in years.

'I have knelt down. My hand is burning so I've stopped the spanking, but I am running my hand over her rump while I slip a finger inside her.'

The waitress behind the counter had turned towards a new customer, and while Rachel whispered to Ryan, she could see the battle that the girl's chest was having beneath her works blouse, not to burst free against the strain.

A fresh gush of pussy juice escaped from Rachel's channel, and she knew she had to finish her kinky commentary fast. 'Her muscles have tightened around my finger, and I'm easing my thumb around so it can push against her nub.' A ripple of intense desire shot from Rachel's chest to her crotch as she kept talking, her voice urgent. 'I'm flicking her clit now, and *oh my God*, she is gonna come! I'm stroking my free hand inside my own knickers so I can rub myself off as well. Fuck, that feels good. You should see her face, she is so beautiful when she's climaxing.'

'Shit, girl.' A suppressed groan issued from Ryan's throat, and for a moment or two the line went faint, as if he could no longer keep his hand on his phone, but had other places where his fingers were needed.

Rachel was surprised to find herself panting, and even more surprised to find herself sat on her own in a busy greasy spoon, the oblivious subject of her shared sexual fantasy now wiping off sticky table tops with an unpleasant-smelling detergent.

'You OK?' Now that he'd come, Ryan's voice had returned to its usual light, casual tone.

Gathering herself together, managing to keep the speed of her pulse and the unexpected need for her boss's touch to herself, Rachel spoke with commendable calm. 'Apart from sitting in a puddle of my own juice, I'm fine. You?'

'Hell yes. I knew you'd be good at this. I have just come like you wouldn't believe.'

Infused with a perverse pride at having made Ryan shoot his load by the force of their combined imaginations alone, Rachel asked, 'So, where are you?'

'Lay-by on the A4. I'm on my way to paint a kitchen.'

'A lay-by? You're kidding me!'

'Nope, I just came all over the kerb.'

'Really?'

Ryan laughed down the phone, 'Yes, really. Look, I have to go now - but I look forward to hearing from you very, very soon.'

The phone went dead, and Rachel cradled it in her hands for a few seconds, staring into the still full, but now cold mug of tea. Her crotch felt hot, and her hands felt cold. She had never wanted sex more. Not daring to risk eye contact with the waitress in case she could somehow read her mind, Rachel put the correct money for her drink on the table and headed outside.

The air felt as though it was teasing her flesh. Leaning back against a nearby lamp post, Rachel fumbled in her pocket, and took out her mobile. Well, he had said he wanted to hear from her very soon.

Got sodden pussy. Had to leave cafe cos couldn't stop looking at waitress. You are a dirty sod.

Heading towards the little office where she worked for Ryan's small painting and decorating business, between 11 o'clock and 2 o'clock every day, Rachel tried to clear her mind and concentrate on the pile of filing and letters that would be waiting for her attention. But Rachel found her eyes kept glancing at her mobile. At the forefront of her mind was Ryan, with his emulsion-spattered overalls and his wicked smile, and her body's requirement for some satisfaction of its own.

The text came through as she sat at her little desk.

At 2pm I will text you again. No wanking off in the meantime!

Rachel swallowed hard for the second time that day, and

the pulse that had calmed from a sprint to a race in her chest suddenly skyrocketed. Squeezing her legs together, she desperately tried to deny her need to wank. She had always fancied Ryan a bit, but she had never believed he could make her feel like this.

It had been three days ago, when Rachel had been having a moan to her boss about how she really needed to earn some extra money. Ryan had been sympathetic to her need to pay the bills, but had shaken his head, saying he'd happily employ her for more hours, but he simply didn't have the additional work for her to do. She could already do everything that was required in her three hours a day. Rachel remembered how Ryan had become quiet then; the flirty banter they'd always shared distant for a moment, until he quietly suggested that maybe she could earn some money from him in a totally different way.

He hadn't asked her to sleep with him for money, but had suggested that maybe she would like to give him text sex, phone sex, something good to think about when he was painting endless stretches of magnolia onto pensioner's walls. "A perk of the job", he'd called it.

She'd laughed, embarrassed - but he'd known she was interested. Something about Ryan's proposition intrigued her, appealing to the naughty streak she had kept to herself for far too long. In the past Rachel had considered making a play for him; but he was her boss, and there had to be rules. Now, however, the rules were being broken - and for the fee of an extra hour's wage a day.

The time at her desk usually flew by. Answering customer calls, arranging quotes for painting jobs, sorting out his chaotic accounts, and singing along to the music on the radio, safe in the knowledge that no one else was being subjected to her awful voice. Today, however, Rachel's work seemed slow and inefficient. Talking sternly to herself, she reminded herself that this was just a business arrangement; and that if it got in the way of her proper work Ryan would get rid of her, and then she'd be in real financial trouble.

After a lifetime, two o'clock came round, and Rachel's mobile beeped into life.

Take your clothes off.

Rachel blinked as she read the text - did she really have to take them off, or was this just pretend?

Are they off yet?

Texting back *Yes,* even though all she had done was remove her jumper, Rachel felt the twitch at her groin remind her of how damp her knickers had been earlier.

Good. Get on your hands and knees in front of the desk.

Sitting cross-legged on the dusty floor carpet, the secretary typed, *Ready.*

In one minute I am going to call you. Place the phone so it can go on to loud speaker - so I can hear you, and you can hear me, but you don't need to use your hands.

A frisson of fresh desire shot up Rachel's spine, and suddenly she realised that she'd been kidding herself. Of course she was going to take her clothes off. Even though it would be easy to just pretend that she was doing what she was told, she wanted to obey his orders.

Removing her clothes with top speed, taking a second to crank up the thermostat on the wall so she didn't freeze to death, Rachel got into the doggy position. Shaking a little as she waited, her blue eyes became fixated on the rectangular phone on the floor between her hands. She willed it to ring before she had time to think about the fact she was being paid to do this.

The phone vibrated into life just as Rachel was brushing a stray hair that had escaped from her russet ponytail from her eyes.

'Can you hear me?'

'Yes.'

'Good.' Ryan's voice echoed a little, and Rachel thought he was probably calling her from the back of his van. 'Now, I want you to do everything I say, and to prove you are doing it, I want you to take a picture with your phone when instructed. Yes?'

Her heart thudding in her neck, Rachel agreed, aware of nothing now but the voice coming through the speaker of the phone before her.

'Right, dirty bitch. Pick up the phone, take a picture of your tits as they hang down, and send it to me. Do it now.'

Rachel picked up the mobile clumsily, and after a few failed attempts at taking a picture he could actually make out as her tits, rather than just an out-of-focus pink blob, she fired it off and placed the phone back down.

Only 30 seconds passed before her boss's voice could be heard faintly muttering sounds of appreciation as he received the shot. 'Excellent - I knew you'd have gorgeous tits. Now, take your right hand and play with your left nipple. Tell me how it feels.'

Obediently, Rachel tweaked her left tip between her fingers, rolling them over and around her breast, 'It feels good. My chest is hard for you. It is enjoying my touch, but it wants your touch.'

'Or maybe the touch of the waitress from this morning?'

'She was hot, but it is your hands I want.'

'Good girl.' She could hear a hint of smugness in his voice, but didn't care. Her right teat was already becoming jealous of the attention that its partner was receiving. Yet it didn't cross her mind to cheat and swap hands and body sides.

'My tit is so tight. And my other one hurts because it isn't being touched.'

'How does your arse feel?'

'Neglected.' With a start, Rachel realised that was the truth. Her bum suddenly felt cold and left out. She wanted a hand to trail over it; to dance carelessly between her legs, squeeze her arse and tease her clit. Her words were rushed and almost angry, as she began to tell him so. 'Do you have any bloody idea how wet I am? How wet I have been since the café this morning. I have hardly got any work done for thinking about you with that girl's mouth around your cock! A cock I haven't even bloody well seen!'

Breathless, her right arm beginning to ache from holding up her whole body, Rachel stopped her rant, but kept her hand teasing her left tit.

Ryan had obviously moved, for the echo around his words had gone as he said, 'Stop playing with your tit. Is it red?'

'Very.' Rachel's left hand returned to the floor with both relief and a surge of frustration.

'Show me.'

Again Rachel fumbled with the camera setting on her phone, and sent him the evidence he wanted to see.

'Beautiful. Now take the ruler off the desk and use it to spank your own arse. I don't care how, just do it. I want to hear the swish as you slap it against your rump. Start now, and don't stop until I tell you. I am going to enjoy listening to you earn your extra wages for a while.'

Gripping the ruler she used to mark her way down the spreadsheets she habitually updated, Rachel awkwardly swung it up and around her, so that she could smack her own backside whilst remaining on all fours. She closed her eyes as she concentrated, the first hit sending small jolts of electricity through her, surprising her with how good it felt to spank yourself, rather than having someone else wield their chosen weapon against your arse.

After a while Rachel began to yelp with every strike, and as she let out a mewl or whine, she could hear Ryan echo her enjoyment, wondering if he was as close to coming as she was, her imagination filling in all the blanks as her head made believe that it was his arm swiping at her butt. That was when she started talking; her desire running away with her mouth.

'I want you here. I want your hand on my arse. I can see your tongue between my legs. I swear I can actually feel it. I can feel you lapping at my nub while I bruise my own backside. I can feel your fingers on my tits. You want them there, don't you? You want to run them over my nipples, don't you? You are a filthy bastard, aren't you!'

She didn't pause long enough for Ryan to actually reply, but the guttural sounds his throat were making down the phone spoke volumes as she continued. 'I bet you'd like to see how red my arse is. It is burning. It is glowing. It hurts, but I don't want the hurt to stop. I can't take a picture, though. I can't reach with the camera. If you want to see how wet I am, how wet you are making me, how swollen my pussy is as I do everything that you tell me to, then you'll have to come and see for yourself.'

Rachel's right arm was getting stiff, so she swapped hands, treating the other half of her butt to the same body-heating pleasure that her left side had received.

So consumed was she in her delicious self-punishment that she didn't hear the door to the office open. She didn't notice that the voice she could hear, breathless and simmering with barely controlled lust, was no longer coming through the speaker on her phone.

'Your wish is my command!' Ryan tore the ruler from Rachel's hand and pushed his startled secretary onto her back.

They stared at each other in total silence for a second. Chests rising and falling in unison as he drank in Rachel's orgied state, and her brain mentally processed the fact that Ryan wasn't a voice on the end of the phone any more.

He strode to her desk, took out an envelope and threw it down at his secretary. 'That is your extra cash for today. For the phone sex, for your incredible dirtiness. Consider yourself paid.'

Ryan pulled off his clothes as he spoke, the smell of paint

and turpentine assaulting Rachel's nostrils as his overalls dropped next to her. 'This, however, is not for money. This is because I have never wanted to fuck anyone so badly in my life. If you don't want me to touch you for real, now is very much the time to say so!'

Rachel reached out her arms and pulled him down, grabbing Ryan's gorgeously rigid cock between her hands; beginning to pump him off while he hunted in his discarded jacket for a condom.

'I guess you could call this a perk to add to the perks of the job?'

She didn't bother replying to him, for Ryan's face was now creased with want as he thumped between her open legs, his fingers grasping Rachel's butt, creating extra shots of pleasure as he gripped her self-inflicted bruises.

Riding him hard, making sure her clit was banging against his body with every contact, Rachel smiled to herself. Every job needed a perk - this one was going to take some beating ...

Passage to Paradise
by Kathleen Tudor

Jenna wiped down the bakery case with a sort of relief, pleased to have survived the afternoon rush for yet another day. She'd quickly learned that, in this business, it was death to try to get between a peckish office worker and her 2 p.m. treats. She was considering a covert pick-me-up of her own when the door chimed, announcing the arrival of her favourite regular, Adam.

He often arrived after the afternoon crush, and as he strode toward her he gave her his boyish smile, completely at odds with the suit he wore so well. 'Adam!' She smiled broadly at him, already reaching for his favourite filled pastry.

'Not today,' he said. 'Just some cookies for the guys. They're throwing me a *bon voyage* party.'

'Oh?' Jenna caught herself wanting to pout, and trod on her own foot under the counter to crush the impulse. 'Are you moving?'

'No, nothing quite so extreme. My company is sending me to Greece for a month to do all the training for a new branch they want to open.' He grinned and added cheekily, 'Sometimes it sucks being the best at what you do!'

Jenna sighed as she bagged two dozen varied cookies. 'That sounds like a dream.'

'This is the villa where we'll be staying.' Adam pulled a brochure from his jacket's inner pocket, and Jenna leant over the counter, accomplishing the twin goals of seeing better and affording Adam an angle down the front of her blouse.

'We?' she asked, idly.

'Yeah, my best friend and I. He's a tech genius, and I convinced the boss that he was the best man to get the technical side of the operation running smoothly.' She snorted, and he shrugged. 'He really will do a perfect job, and I already know we work well together.'

'I wish I knew something about technology. I would do *anything* to live in Greece for a month.'

'Oh sure, you say that,' he teased back, leaning a bit closer over the counter. She blushed as his face closed distance with hers, but she didn't quite step back to reclaim her personal space. Just her luck – the guy was leaving the country, and he chooses *now* to finally flirt back in earnest.

'Do you think you could sneak me into your luggage?'

Adam laughed and straightened, handing her $20 and accepting the bag of cookies without waiting for change. 'Maybe you should come by Fischer's Bar at 8 and see if you can talk me into it,' he said. He started for the door, leaving the open invitation hanging in the air like flour dust.

Jenna counted the minutes until she could close the bakery at 5 p.m.; she closed alone, but it was a more than fair price to pay for not having to come in before dawn like most of the other employees. By the time she was bolting the lock on the back door, her decision was firm – she was going to go to that party, and she was going to see just how serious Adam was with his teasing.

'I am an idiot, and I am completely nuts,' Jenna muttered to herself a little over three hours later. A couple heading her way on the sidewalk gave her a wide berth, and she sighed. She had taken every second she could grab to prepare, not giving herself a chance to really think through what she was doing. Now she was standing outside Fischers in jeans that could have been painted on and a top that showed off her cleavage and flat stomach nearly equally, and she was petrified. Better make a decision before I'm arrested for solicitation, she thought, and, with a heaving sigh, stepped forward and pushed through the door.

Adam's party was the only large group in sight, a mix of handsome young men and gorgeous young women at the back of the bar, laughing loudly and shouting over one another in general good cheer. His back was to her as she approached, but just as she would have hesitated, lost in a sea of strangers, Adam turned and his eyes found her, then widened in appreciation. He traced the long, heavy waves of her hair down to her waist, and she realised he'd only ever seen it bundled up into a bun at the bakery. With a slight smile she shook it out for him, growing confident at the way his mouth pursed in appreciation.

'Hey,' she said, 'hope I'm not too late for all the fun.'

'Not at all.' He led her to the group and introduced her, and she was grateful when he didn't bother to name the numerous strangers surrounding her – it was a ritual she'd always found more terrifying than helpful in a large group of unknowns. Someone offered her a beer and she took it to have something to hold on to. Around her, the group continued to chatter and laugh, including her naturally without the pressure of normal getting-to-know-you interrogation, and she soon felt at ease, sharing amusing stories and laughing along with their jokes.

Adam drifted through the group, pausing here and there for conversation and then moving on, but she felt his eyes on her back often, and if she turned she could usually catch his eye and his quick smile. She considered getting up and going to him, but he took the decision out of her hands a moment later, appearing at her shoulder. 'Are you having a good time?' he asked.

'Your friends are great,' she replied, her voice pitched for his ears only. She'd let go of her stupid idea of seducing him soon after she'd joined the crowd, and felt comfortable and relaxed instead, glad not to have the insane plan weighing on her.

'They're also loud,' he said back. 'Would you like to talk?' He offered her his hand and she took it, expecting him to lead the way to the bar or to a distant booth. Instead he headed toward a hallway in the back, pausing before an unmarked door. 'Sort of a VIP room,' he said, and flashed a key before letting her in.

The room was not huge, but it was certainly comfortable, and the couches, arranged for conversation, were plush and inviting. She stepped in past him and admired the cool lighting and sensual décor. 'I have a question for you,' he said as he shut the door.

'Hmmm?'

'Did you mean what you said about going to Greece?' he asked.

'You mean about wanting to go?'

'I mean about doing anything to get there,' he said, and this time he stepped so close that she was forced to tilt her head back to meet his eyes.

'What do you want?' she whispered, a shiver of fear tracing her spine.

'I'm not going to hurt you,' he murmured. He stepped around her, behind her, and his hands came to rest lightly on her shoulders. 'You're very beautiful, Jenna. I think it would be nice to bring you to Greece with me. More than nice.' His hands stroked up her neck, and she shuddered. 'But I don't want to force you to do anything you don't want to do.'

Jenna took a deep breath. Imagining was one thing, but could this possibly be happening? And if it was, did she really want it to? Truly? The answer hit her like lightning, and she felt her pussy throb with sudden heaviness and moisture. 'Sex with a guy I'm attracted to and a month in paradise? Where's the downside?' she asked, her voice going deep with excitement. She turned toward him and found his eyes sparkling with pleasure, but a certain note of caution still showed in a certain tension around the edges.

Adam leant down slowly and brushed his lips against hers in a shock of tingling pleasure. 'But that's the thing,' he said. 'It's never that easy, is it?' He backed away slightly and turned toward the door, and Jenna deflated, desperate to know what she'd done to disappoint him. But when he opened the door, the hallway wasn't empty. Adam stepped aside, and a tall, lean man with an athletic build stepped into the room, eyeing her with pleasure. 'Thing is, we like to share.'

'The best friend,' Jenna realised.

'Nate,' the athlete said. He put out his hand, and when she reached for it automatically, he kissed the back of her hand. She shivered.

'You can still leave, Jenna,' Adam whispered from behind her. She jumped – she had been so focused on the other man, she hadn't seen him move. She gave a long, shuddering exhale. One the one hand, she was terrified. On the other, she'd never been this aroused in her life. One hand, still clasped with Nate's, his hot gaze on her. In the other hand …

Jenna reached back slowly, deliberately, and rested her hand on the erection that strained Adam's slacks. She tightened her grip on Nate's hand, pulling him closer, and with that, four hot hands and two mouths were on her, caressing and teasing in a dance that was like nothing she'd ever felt before. Awash in sensation, she could only stand there and let the men arouse and entice her.

After a several moments of bliss, hands and tongues vanished, and Jenna swayed, bereft. 'Intense, isn't it?' Adam asked. He started to move around her, and Nate moved in the same direction so that they remained on opposite sides of her.

'Pretty Jenna … Do you think you can handle it?'

'Two men?'

'A whole month …'

Nate was behind her now, and Jenna leant back, knowing instinctively that he would be there, alert to her smallest movements and ready to steady her with his own athletic body. 'I can more than handle it,' she said, her voice coming out so husky she hardly recognised it. Her panties were soaked through, and she wouldn't be shocked if her jeans were getting damp.

Adam stepped forward until her body was pressed between both of theirs, and Jenna's breath was coming in quick pants of excitement. 'My buddy, Nate here, would really like to fuck you,' he said. Jenna whimpered as her clit seemed to twitch against the tight fabric.

'And while I'm doing that, Adam would love it if you'd suck his cock,' Nate said from behind her. His erection was pressed firmly into her ass, and she could also feel Nate's straining against her belly.

'But if you don't want to do those things, right here, right now, then you should leave. Because Greece is going to be way too much to handle if you don't even want tonight.'

She'd almost forgotten about Greece. To prove it, Jenna decided that actions would speak louder than words. She dropped to her knees in front of Adam, and her fingers tore at his pants until his cock sprung free. As she sucked it into her mouth, both she and Adam released pent-up moans of pleasure and desire.

'That's fucking hot,' Nate said. He knelt behind her and pushed her tiny top up and out of the way. Adam rested a hand on her hair and watched as his friend squeezed and fondled her breasts, displaying them for Adam's enjoyment and tweaking her nipples to elicit little whimpers and moans. Her heart was pounding as she sucked Adam's cock, feeling his hands stroking through her hair as another pair did wicked things to her breasts. 'Do you still want to go on?'

Jenna moaned loudly in assent, arching her back to press her ass more firmly into Nate. He laughed. 'Adam, go have a seat and let me get this girl properly attired for the occasion.' She wanted to protest as the generous cock was pulled slowly away from her teasing lips and tongue. Giving head was always fun because she knew how much the guys liked to watch, and double the audience meant double the pleasure for her.

As Adam crossed the room and sprawled on one of the sofas, Nate gently helped her to her feet. Still behind her, he started by kneeling and lifting each leg in turn to remove her shoes and toss them aside. Adam smiled as he watched her, and she smiled back, feeling gorgeous as he kicked out of his pants and wrapped a fist around his own cock. He stroked slowly as Nate pulled her shirt out of the way and tossed it aside, and her cunt pulsed with his rhythm.

Nate's hands rose again to knead her breasts and Jenna let her head fall back with a sigh of pleasure at the sensation. After a moment they drifted lower, trailing goosebumps down her ribs until he reached the waistband of her jeans. With a "pop", the button released and Nate was peeling the jeans down over her legs and helping her out of them. She stood with her legs slightly spread, knowing what was coming next, and wasn't disappointed when Nate reached around in front of her to dip two fingers into the pool of moisture between her legs.

They both moaned as his hand found the slickness there, and he rewarded her arousal with a couple of circles around her clit before he lifted his hand to show off the shining wetness to Adam, whose eyes glinted as he stroked himself. 'This may be the wettest woman I have ever seen,' Nate said, his voice nearly a moan.

'Then how about you get that mouth of hers back over here and give her what she wants,' Adam suggested, and Jenna didn't bother waiting for a second invitation. She knelt in front of the couch, deliberately raising her ass to display herself for Nate as she sucked Adam's cock deep into her throat and was rewarded by his almost-shout. She sucked eagerly, her head bobbing, but Adam grabbed her by the hair and slowed her down. 'Easy, baby, we've got time,' he said.

She hadn't heard Nate undress, but she heard the rip of a condom packet, and a moment later she felt him kneel behind her, position himself at the mouth of her hungry pussy, and then, with a grunt, he thrust home and drove himself deep inside her. She couldn't help the deep, throaty moan that escaped her, and the vibrations in her throat triggered a similar moan in Adam. Nate's cock was thick, and she couldn't help squeezing her body around the filling sensation.

Nate grabbed her hips and used the leverage to slam into her twice, fast, before settling on a slow, steady rhythm. 'This is definitely the wettest pussy I have ever fucked,' he said, and Jenna purred her pleasure at the compliment.

'Not bad with the mouth either,' Adam replied. He tightened his grip on her hair, and Jenna whimpered happily at the sensation. Her pussy clenched, and Nate groaned, grinding into her before resuming his rhythm. As Adam held her head still, he thrust up slowly, fucking her face in the hottest way Jenna had ever experienced. She clenched her pussy again; she was so close she could taste it, and every teasing stroke to her throat and cunt was driving her crazy.

'Look at her squirm,' Nate said. 'I think she likes it.'

'Go ahead, bro, make her come. I want to watch.'

Jenna moaned before Nate's hand even moved, and the moment his fingers found her clit, she bucked into them, nearly screaming onto Adam's cock as her whole body throbbed convulsively with pleasure. Nate kept up his steady thrusts, drawing out the waves of pleasure for her as she continued to moan and suck. Adam, who had slowed his thrusts into her mouth while she came, started to fuck her mouth in earnest as she drifted back down from the pinnacle of pleasure.

'Fuck yes,' Adam said, and then Jenna felt a shudder go through him a moment before he arched up, buried his cock in her throat, and roared with pleasure. She took him deep into her throat, swallowing around his cock until he was completely spent. She smiled up at him, and he grabbed her gently by the hair to pull her up into a hot kiss.

Nate slammed into her harder as her tongue danced with Adam's, surprising her, and she moaned as the movement sent a few extra tingles through her clit. Adam sucked her tongue into his mouth and bit down gently as Nate slammed into her again, his pace getting faster and harder until all three of them were moaning in excitement. When he came, his fingers dug deep into her hips and she broke from Adam, to cry out in her own pleasure. He nibbled at her neck as both she and Nate panted.

A moment later she felt Nate move away, and Adam pulled her up onto the couch. She was soon nestled between the two sated men, each of whom idly stroked whatever bit of her skin was closest to hand. She shivered a little as her exhausted body responded to the light touches.

'So, beautiful, think you can keep up a pace like that for a month?' Adam asked, a note of teasing in his voice.

'That depends,' she answered, smiling. 'Do you two think you can keep up with *me*?'

'Pack your bags, you little nymph,' Nate said on a laugh. 'It's going to be one hell of a vacation.'

But why let it end there? Jenna thought, and drew Nate down for another sizzling kiss.

Coming While Going ...
by Marlene Yong

Dextra had been preoccupied all evening. Usually she played a savage game, leaving at least a couple of us 20, maybe even 30, quid down. Tonight, though, she'd dropped 50 in less than an hour and when she raised Harriet with only a pair of eights we knew something was up. And Harriet, no bluffer, had been grinning broadly since her cards were dealt. She had three queens.

'What's up, Dextra?' I asked. She was toying with a brown leather pocket book, repeatedly flipping it open and sliding her fingers inside as if searching for a mislaid lottery ticket.

Dextra shrugged. 'Just deal!' she ordered me.

We all stared at her. For Dextra not to unburden her soul verged on the apocalyptic.

There was a haunted look in her eye I'd only seen once before – when some sod she'd trotted round after like a constipated poodle for several months had buggered off with a heavily made-up tart from Fulham. Any guy who could ditch Dextra had to be something pretty special.

Out of the four of us who met every week to trade anecdotes, have a few drinks and a friendly game of cards, Dextra was by far the sexiest. And the one who pulled most often. Her past and origins were something of a mystery. She was beautiful with oriental-European features, a soft, sinuous body and a mildly olive skin. She could have passed as Vietnamese or Filipina. Like many semi-orientals she was diminutive. Guys found her shapely legs, high breasts, and rich, exotic scent irresistible. None of us knew her original name: we simply called her Dextra as a result of an accident.

Each week, with inscrutable features, she regaled us with some new story of a sexual conquest. At the punchline she'd burst out giggling like a little girl. This evening she acted moody and truculent.

When I failed to move, she glared at me, scooped together the cards on the table and shoved them at me. 'Deal!' she rasped. I didn't.

Finally her shoulders drooped. 'OK, OK,' she sighed. 'I'll tell you about it. Remember I worked in Paris for several weeks? Well, one day …

It was a muggy Parisian afternoon. Dextra's sweat-drenched blouse clung to her in dark patches, stimulating her nipples. Which was especially frustrating for she'd sworn to stay celibate whenever she was on a job. A fortnight now and she was getting hornier by the hour.

She was still trying to get used to the Metro and the long, exhausting walks between connections. The weight of her shoulder bag on long leather straps certainly didn't help.

She'd chosen to take the R.E.R. from Etoile to Nation because of its comparatively luxurious coaches. But she hadn't expected that at 5.15 she'd find herself pressed up against the wall of the carriage by grim-faced commuters heading home towards the outer suburbs.

Her work in Paris was proving nowhere as profitable as she'd hoped and she was estimating how soon she could return to England when a hunk with craggy features and penetrating azure eyes squeezed in, trapping her against the carriage wall. As his hard body plastered against her, she became aware of an expensive aftershave mixed with a not unpleasant aroma of perspiration. He was only slightly taller but she could tell by the muscles which bulged his tailored linen shirt that he worked out regularly.

Like any metropolitan underground passenger she gazed stoically into space above his shoulder, not acknowledging his existence. She felt his eyes drift down to her body and the familiar tingle of excitement ticked between her thighs. Due to the oppressive heat she had left the top three buttons of the silken blouse undone. She sensed the man savouring the clear vista of her breasts pushed up taut above the flimsy material.

She heard his breath catch as he took in the smoothness of her flesh, which overflowed the cleavage with each judder of the swaying carriage. She regretted he couldn't see her bare legs which she loved to expose. Guessing at the testosterone-triggered turmoil in his loins, her lips bowed in a tiny, knowing smile.

The train swept round a bend in the tunnel and centrifugal force thrust his hips tighter against hers. A moment later Dextra became conscious of something that slithered against her groin. Her heart pounded. For an exhilarating moment she hoped he was pressing an erection against her in spite of her vow to stay celibate. Nevertheless, she jumped with shock as something nudged up the hem of her short, buttoned skirt and forced its way between her legs.

Without moving, she let her inner thighs make a few deductions as to the shape and size of the exploring object. Yes, she concluded. It was a hand, large and bony, but oh, so skilful! Languorously, almost casually, one finger tugged her knickers to one side and another finger located and rotated her clit. Instantly her labia unfurled and gaped. With only the minutest shift of her head and eyes she assessed the passengers on either side. None of them could have reached across unseen to fumble under her skirt. So it must be …

She jabbed a peek at the man's face. He gave no sign that he was her anonymous groper. From the corner of her eye she studied him. Moderately good-looking, clean cut, well dressed in quality jeans and the linen shirt. Maybe a little conventional but exuding an aura of sex. Dextra forced herself to breathe steadily. Only by biting the inside of her lip could she stop herself thrusting her hips forward to frot his probing digits. The pressure on her clitoris was becoming irresistible. She regretted her intention to forgo sex until she returned to England. If it was on offer, why look a gift horse …? If anyone could satisfy her immediate needs, it might as well be him.

Having settled the matter, Dextra saw no point in subtlety. Taking the initiative, she slid her left hand up between his pants legs. He did not react except to fix her with the azure, penetrating gaze. She urgently wanted him to tug at her nipples, which jutted, hard and purple, in outline against the fabric. Instead, she scuttled her fingers up his fly, located and slid open his zip. Insinuating her fingers, she eased her hand inside. It was difficult with bodies wedged on either side but eventually she managed to reach the man's cock, trapped inside his cotton underpants, and stroked it upwards, her thumb on one side and forefinger on the other. It soon repaid her by stiffening to its full length.

Deftly Dextra extracted his twitching organ through the gap in his underpants. It stirred restlessly against her pleated skirt. Her clutching fingers froze around his shaft as the carriage burst from the tunnel into the glaring platform lights of the Gare de Lyon. The doors rumbled open and the train disgorged 90 per cent of its passengers like a tree shaking loose its leaves in a strong wind.

Somehow, though, the man kept himself pressed against her. His hard-on, unwilling to shrink, even from embarrassment, managed to hide from view in her firm clasp and the folds of her skirt.

A swarm of new commuters streamed into the carriage. This time the throng jammed the two of them against the wall of the compartment next to the door on Dextra's left. Luckily her massive shoulder bag hid the lower halves of their torsos from view on her right.

Dextra was moist already. So moist the man could slide

two fingers into her with ease. Then his mouth was touching her ear and his tongue was darting inside it. Unconsciously she lifted her knee and rested it against his hip, which opened her sex wider. He removed his fingers and substituted his thumb, which was quickly engulfed in secretions.

Meanwhile Dextra was squeezing and relaxing her grip on his cock in a parody of a vagina in the throes of orgasm. Not enough to bring him off, but so stimulating it goaded him to ram his glans against her crotch.

For the first time Dextra looked into his eyes and found herself gazing back into blue liquid spheres and was lost. Abruptly he eased his thumb from her gaping cunt and manoeuvred his cock against her labia.

Surely he wasn't going to … Not here in a crowded train! But he was. And he did. She wriggled her hips and thighs to accommodate him and unexpectedly he was fluming into her. He hardly needed to thrust. His shaft surged forward, a lethal shark nosing through a headily scented creek to nudge against a soft but unyielding embankment.

Her breathing quickened. She felt her skin flush. Instinctively she bent her knee to push downwards onto the top of his shaft and frot her clitoris against it. His hands were everywhere, on her thighs, her breasts, gripping her buttocks and pulling her towards him to grind his crotch against her, oblivious to the bemused stares of the Gallic passengers peering round to discover the source of the frenetic activity by the door.

Dextra, who hadn't so much as spoken to a guy since she'd left London a fortnight before, couldn't stave off her climax. Her vaginal tunnel rippled spasmodically as the man's loins slapped against hers in abrasive jerks.

Trembling, she lowered her left leg, which still nestled against his right hip. Through a haze she saw his gaze slide away to peer out the window at the lights of Nation now blossoming rapidly into view. He swung his body away from her to face the door, zipping up his pants as he did so. In a daze, Dextra scrabbled to button up the opening in the front of her skirt in full sight of several wide-eyed straphangers, some of whose expressions morphed from indignation to envy as they noticed the wet streaks already darkening the material.

The tidal wave of new commuters forced her backwards away from the door as she tried to alight. As the door slammed she caught sight of the man receding down the platform towards the exit. The train began to move. But something wasn't right. She lowered her bag from her shoulder and ...

'You mean he actually ...?' Harriet couldn't finish the sentence she was so gobsmacked.

Dextra nodded, her eyes afire. 'While he was inside me he just unzipped my bag and lifted everything I had. Luckily I'd left my special purse with my credit cards, passport and return air ticket back at the hotel. All I had on me was about 30 quid in Euros I'd picked up that morning. Otherwise I'd have been in real trouble. What a bastard!' she murmured moodily. Then, sighing, added, 'I could marry a bloke like that. He's everything I've ever dreamt of. Good-looking, talented ... I would have tried to trace him but - well, who could I ask?'

Her eyes flicked from one to another of us, not really expecting an answer.

'But didn't you suspect *anything*?' I exclaimed.

'Why should I? How could I have guessed he was only after my money?'

Surely that wasn't Dextra talking? A crummy old music hall joke?

But I was beginning to understand. 'You said you ... had your *left* hand round his cock?'

For the first time that evening Dextra allowed herself a sour grin. Years ago a joyrider had smashed into her, leaving the nerves in her left hand seriously weakened. It had also endowed her with her nickname, Dextra: the right-handed one.

'Which means,' I deduced, 'that your right hand, your working hand, was free?'

Morosely Dextra flicked open the brown leather pocket book with which she'd been playing all evening and pulled out a thick wad of notes, which she ribbon-spread on the table. We all stared, mesmerised. Apart from a few 20s in sterling, there was a mass of high-denomination Euros.

'He had about 900 quid in this,' she said dejectedly. 'It was in his back pocket. But no address, no telephone number.' Her voice faltered. 'Fucking heartbreaking. If he could lift this amount in just one morning from tourists on the Metro, what couldn't we have achieved together, me and him?'

'You mean -' Harriet gasped '- while you were having a public knee-trembler, you were actually dipping him?'

Dextra glared at her self-righteously. 'Of course. Business is business!'

Show No Mercy
by Giselle Renarde

As a paying customer, Simon could do as he pleased.

Everything was so different now, so different than it had been back when they were dating. That seemed like for ever ago. Mercedes couldn't even remember what she'd seen in Simon in the first place. He was an old man – at least, he was older than she was – though his body didn't show it. When they'd been together like that, like an almost-real couple, he'd been sophisticated. He'd been suave. He'd reminded her of Cary Grant – yes, that's why she'd fallen for him back in those days, and fallen so hard she didn't even care that he was married to some old broad named Florence.

'Remind me: when's the wedding?' Simon sat right smack in the middle of her loveseat, one leg crossed over the other. What a smug bastard he'd become since they'd broken up.

'Fuck off,' Mercedes replied. She wasn't getting into this with him. Not now, not ever.

Simon didn't react to the insult. 'Coming up pretty soon, isn't it?' He nodded in the direction of the goddamn video game console Anwar had hooked up to her TV. 'Moving his stuff in already, I see. What's this guy's name again? Anwar bin Laden?'

'Didn't I just tell you to fuck off?' Mercedes didn't want to lose her temper completely, but she'd found lately that the sex was much better when Simon got arrogant and she got angry.

So, yeah, it was a definite turn-on when Simon said, 'And I bet you'll still let me fuck you when you're a married woman. You will, won't you? I'm sure you've thought about it.'

Mercedes said nothing. Leaning her ass back against the retro sideboard she was using as a TV stand, she perceived the brush of her clothing against her flesh. God, she wished she was naked already. She wanted him to throw her down on that loveseat and just fuck the life out of her.

'This is quite a secret to keep from your husband-to-be,' Simon went on. His tone was irreproachably casual, like all these weighty matters were of no consequence to her. Like opening his mouth to the wrong person wouldn't ruin her life. But, then, he was married too …

'This is quite a secret to keep from your wife,' Mercedes shot back. 'What do you think she'd say if she knew you were paying me to fuck you? This pretty young thing having sex with her husband, and all for cash. How would she like that?'

Back when they were "dating" or whatever you'd call it – back before money was changing hands – Simon always got riled up when Mercedes mentioned his wife. Now he took everything in stride. Nothing seemed to matter any more.

Rising from the loveseat, Simon crossed the narrow expanse of her living room and took her arms in his tight grip, holding them firmly against her sides. 'You know what I'm going to do to you today?' His breath was hot on her ear, his voice still calm.

'No.' Mercedes was a brat with him now. 'I wish you'd tell me so we could damn well get it over with. I want to rid this place of your stench before Anwar comes over.'

Simon laughed, a piercing cackle. 'Stench? What could he possibly smell over the stink of your cunt?'

His grip on her arms was tighter now, but she didn't struggle. 'How about the heady perfume of failure, old age, and disappointment coming off you?'

When Simon pressed his body up against hers, she held on tight to the sideboard for fear she'd knock down the TV if she tumbled backwards. His cock was already thick with arousal, and the feel of it against her pelvis sent a swift heat soaring through her body. Her pussy fluttered in anticipation.

'My only disappointment,' he said, 'is that I let myself fuck a dirty whore.'

Mercedes pressed in against his heat, until her clothed breasts were flat against his chest. Her face was at the height of his armpit when she said, 'I was never a whore until you made me one.'

'But you were always dirty.' Without warning, he pulled her across the room and shoved her down on the loveseat. Her knees met the cushion first, and she somehow ended up with both hands on the armrest and her butt in the air. 'You've got a big ass, Mercy.'

That panged, but only for a moment. 'Yeah, and you love it.'

'If only your tits were this big.' He hiked her skirt up over her waist and kneaded her ass with both hands. She didn't usually wear a thong, but with Simon she tried a lot of things she didn't usually do.

'My tits are big enough.' Mercedes could barely think, much less speak, as Simon ran his hot hands in circles around her butt cheeks.

'Unbutton your sweater,' he said. 'Let me feel.'

'It's a cardigan.' The only way to undo the buttons in that position was to lean her forearms against the side of the loveseat. This freed up her fingers, and she worked as fast as she could because she couldn't wait a second longer to feel his sizzling skin against hers.

Simon pulled Mercy's tits out roughly from inside her lace-trimmed camisole. She'd taken her bra off the second she got home and picked up the voicemail that he was coming over. It was brutishly presumptuous of Simon to stop by as he wished, telling instead of asking first. He wouldn't be able to do that once she was married to Anwar, that was for damn sure.

'Not so big.' Simon grabbed one breast and then the other, squeezing in that beastly manner born of entitlement. 'I always wished you had huge tits, so big they made you slump over.'

Mercedes knew better than to be insulted by this. 'So find yourself another whore. Get one with a giant rack, if you can afford her.'

His hand came down hard across her backside. The shock of this action trapped Mercy's breath in her lungs, and she struggled to recover. She couldn't let on how much pleasure-pain that one surprise spanking generated in her body.

'I don't want another whore,' Simon said simply, like he was turning away a second helping of dessert. 'I want my Mercy.'

Another blow landed firm against her cheek, and she turned in time to watch her flesh wobble. She couldn't believe it was red already, just in that one spot where his palm had landed. Rosy red on a sea of gold. Her ass was pretty big, but so what? Simon liked it, Anwar liked it, and, most importantly, she liked it. What else mattered?

Simon pinched her nipple and twisted, like he was revving up the engine on his stupid old Mustang. He was such a middle-aged stereotype, though in some people's books he was past middle age. Still, he knew just what to do to get her pussy dripping with desire. When he smacked her ass again, a bolt of electricity travelled straight to the nipple between his fingers before her clit exploded like fireworks.

'Fuck!' Mercedes moaned, almost inaudibly, but of course Simon heard.

'What's that?' he asked. His voice was wicked sometimes, like the bad guy in a Disney movie. 'You want me to fuck you?'

'God, yes!' It was out before she could stop it, but who would she have been kidding if she'd said no? 'Please fuck me, Simon. I need it.'

Releasing his grasp on one nipple, Simon fished for the other. He rolled that pebbled flesh between his thumb and forefinger, increasing the pressure with each pass. 'I think I like this better,' he said. 'I enjoy watching you squirm.'

'You're an asshole!' she shot back, though her insult was interrupted by another blow to her red flesh. 'Fuck ...' Mercedes let her head collapse onto the loveseat's arm. Everything in her apartment felt trashy when Simon was here. She felt trashy, too.

'Who's the paying customer?' Another spank struck her ass, and another, and a quick third. 'This is not about what you want, Mercy.'

She hissed as her butt cheeks burned. How could his hands be so hot? Didn't it hurt him when he struck her? Because it sure as hell hurt Mercedes. Her ass was sizzling, stinging, with a funny prickle like tiny raindrops falling against her skin.

Every statement Simon offered presented her an opportunity to argue, or not to argue. This time, she chose the latter. 'Fine.' Her voice was hoarse with the pain he'd callously inflicted. 'What do you want, then? You know you can have it.'

He smacked her ass right along the crack, where it didn't hurt so much. His other hand retreated from her chest. 'Do you have any balloons?' he asked her.

'Balloons?' What the hell did he want balloons for? 'Yeah, from Anwar's birthday party. Why?'

When she finally looked up into his face, she found him grinning, wolf-like, ear to ear. Why did that appeal to her?

'Get them,' he said. 'Get two and fill them up with water, then put them down the front of your top.'

Now she understood, and for a long moment she wasn't

sure if she should feel turned on or insulted. He backed away from her, and she would have sat down if she thought her raging cheeks could handle it.

'Well? What are you waiting for?'

Mercedes shifted from the loveseat, her skirt tumbling down to cover her legs. Her unappreciated breasts sunk into her camisole as she walked to the linen closet and rifled through wrapping paper and gift tags. When she'd found the dollar store balloons, she plucked out two clear ones dotted with silver stars and filled them pretty full in the bathroom sink.

Without emotion, Mercedes tied up her balloons. What was Simon doing all this time? Was he standing in the hallway watching her? She couldn't bear to turn around and look, but she was sure she could feel his gaze sweeping down her skirt. He was like an animal these days, always stalking, prowling, hunting her as prey.

Her camisole was made of stretchy cotton and it had a sort of built-in bra, a strip of elastic that clung tight around the body, just below her breasts. The water she'd run into her silver star balloons had been warm, yet they burned her poor nipples when she dropped them into her top. Mercedes watched herself in the mirror, fiddling with her makeshift prosthetics until the ties faced front like hard little nubs. God, these boobs were huge. *Huge*.

The stars weren't visible through the white fabric of her camisole, but the balloons themselves overshot the lace. Mercedes had to button her thin purple cardigan all the way up to the top to conceal the fake boobs pressed flush to her real ones. Why did he want this so badly? Though, she had to admit, the feel of those hot balloons against her tender, tortured breasts was making her pussy drool against the small triangle of underwear between her thighs. Even though her cardigan was stretched to its limits between those mother-of-pearl buttons, she knew Simon would look at her and see a porn star. She couldn't wait to show him.

When she turned around and he wasn't there, Mercy's heart slunk down into her belly. Why hadn't he been watching and waiting? This was all for him. And then Mercedes heard the footsteps coming from her bedroom. When Simon emerged, he was carrying the long mirror that hung behind her closet door, and she had to hop out of the way or risk him walking straight into her. They'd been a couple, of sorts, so he knew where things were and he took liberties.

It wasn't until Simon had perched her mirror against the loveseat-adjacent wall that he turned around to get a load of Mercedes. His eyebrows rose approvingly, and she knew he didn't mean to let that happen, or to let his jaw swing wide open the way it did. They shared this visceral reaction to one another's bodies. It was an attraction that couldn't be tamped down by time apart, much less relationships with other people. Her body wanted Simon inside it, and the sweet anticipation of a cash reward only sweetened the dirty deal.

'Is this what you want?' Mercedes asked. 'Am I a good whore now?'

Instead of answering, he kissed her, which was a bit of a shock because he almost never kissed her any more. It was rough, this kiss. Simon's tongue felt sharp against hers, like a snake's, but she couldn't have stomached a tender kiss from Simon. Not any more. Again, he gripped her forearms so tightly she'd be lucky to get away without bruises, and he pulled her in close. Her breasts met his chest before she expected them to. They were so goddamn big now that she felt like she had no control over her body. Warm water enveloped in latex caressed her flesh, gobbling up her actual breasts until they became a part of her, at least for the moment. The constraint felt weird, but it felt good. It felt good to be desired the way Simon desired her, like a meaty possession.

'The mirror?' she asked, though she knew well what it

was there for.

He confirmed her suspicion: 'I want to watch.'

The gravel in his voice weakened her knees, but she didn't allow herself to tumble toward the couch until she'd hiked her skirt up above her waist, hooked her thumbs around the waistband on her thong, and shoved it down to her ankles. Simon growled as he watched Mercedes position herself on the loveseat, and her breaths grew ragged when he lost his pants to the floor. He didn't waste any time situating himself behind her, and it wasn't until he grabbed hold of her ass that she realised the flesh was still tender.

In the mirror, they didn't seem to be missing any clothing at all. Mercedes' fake tits were completely enveloped by her cardigan, and Simon hadn't bothered removing his pale blue button-down shirt. Their lower halves weren't visible in the glass, and Mercedes had to turn her head to get a good look at Simon's hand guiding a huge erection into her wet hole. She moaned as his fat cockhead disappeared inside her, followed swiftly by a shaft that seemed to get bigger every time it fucked her.

'You bastard,' she moaned as he filled her full up.

Clinging to her hips, Simon rammed into her. 'Am I?'

'Fuck, yes.'

He pummelled her pussy so hard it panged deep inside and she cringed, her muscles tightening around his shaft, hugging it. 'Am I cruel to you, Mercy?'

'Oh, God …' She tried to adapt to the pain because she knew very well she couldn't tell him to stop. If only she could bring her thighs tight together, but Simon had situated himself between her legs and there was little chance he'd abandon that position. 'You're killing me…'

As she watched a canine grin bleed across his lips, Mercy's pussy began to tremor around his thick shaft. All at once, the pang inside was gone and she felt like she could take him as deep as he wanted to go.

Releasing her hip with one hand, Simon grabbed hold of

Mercedes' shoulder and thrust in her deeply, repeatedly, unrelentingly. The heavy mass of her fake tits coupled with her real ones, and they swung pendulously from her body. The constriction of tight clothing, of breathless latex against her skin, made her gasp, and still she bucked back into the saddle of Simon's hips. She wanted more and more, more than she should take and probably more than he was able to give.

It never felt like fucking an old man, with Simon. His face had those tell-tale wrinkles around the eyes and his lips were probably thinner than they had been in better days, but that man was always hard the instant she walked in the room. To Mercedes, nothing else mattered. The measure of a man's attraction was quite simply his dick. If it was long and strong for her, she knew he was into it.

'God, those tits, Mercy.' Simon grabbed both her shoulders now and reamed her wet cunt. 'Play with your tits, babe. I want to watch you touch them.'

It was hard to move with him fucking her so hard, sending her hurdling over the edge of the loveseat with every thrust, but she managed to rest her sternum against the arm. Simon groaned like he was about to come when she circled her hands around her massive balloon-breasts. She pressed them together beneath her top and was surprised that she could actually feel the pressure of the water against her real boobs, buried deep underneath all that warmth and latex. When she tweaked the ties that acted as substitute nipples, Simon grabbed her black hair in his fist. Even as she shrieked, he didn't seem to realise the pain he caused her, and his negligence, or apathy, or whatever drove him to mistreat her without remorse only encouraged her to buck back harder against him.

Those fake tits bounced wildly as Simon pulled on Mercy's hair like a thick rope, and their reflection in the mirror put her over the edge. He'd never been like this when they were a couple. Anwar was never like this now. She couldn't love a man and let him treat her this way, despite the part of her that so loved to get her ass spanked and her hair pulled and her body insulted and her pussy fucked hard. This could only happen now, with Simon, because there was a part of her that truly hated him.

'Come, you bastard!' Mercedes hugged her massive tits tight to her chest. 'Just fucking fill me with come and get out of my goddamn house!'

Simon wrapped her rope of hair tighter around his hand. 'Come inside a dirty whore?'

'I'm only a whore to you,' she replied, her voice stretched tight by her strained position.

When their eyes met in the mirror, Mercedes tried to escape his gaze, but she found herself transfixed. For a long moment, they stopped moving completely. Her back was arched though she was on her knees, and the pose made her feel like a Sphinx with giant breasts. They quaked with each breath, and as she watched Simon's expressions contort in the mirror, her pussy spasmed around his thick cock. He was coming right now, and she couldn't move a muscle. All she could do was watch his forehead wrinkle, his eyes squint, and his mouth open in a stupor until his pleasure moved through her body and she could feel it too.

Hugging her enormous tits, Mercedes held utterly still as her pussy milked Simon's cock. She could have sworn she could feel the warm jets of come spilling into her cunt, spurt after spurt. They seemed to go on for ever. Or maybe she was imagining things. It didn't matter. She derived pleasure from his pleasure, as much in her body as it was in her mind. Her pussy hugged his spent shaft tight because that was the closest to cuddling they were likely to come, at least today. Anwar would be here soon. Every time, she let herself cut it closer and closer. Maybe she wanted to get caught. Psychology types are always saying people want to get caught. Who knows? They might be right.

Simon pulled out of her and smacked her thigh with his

wet dick a few times before climbing back into his pants. Mercedes could barely take her eyes off her reflection, but she forced herself into her thong while Simon made his way to the door.

'Aren't we forgetting a little something?' she asked, as if he could possibly forego this step.

'Forget?' he scoffed, taking his wallet from his pocket. 'This is my favourite part.'

Mercedes laid her palm flat like Judy Jetson and watched Simon count the bills out into her hand. She wondered if the grin flashing across her lips right now was half as canine as Simon's had been earlier. He tried to bring her down a peg by saying, 'For the honeymoon fund,' but nothing could put a damper on this exchange. Sometimes Mercedes thought she loved Simon's money more than she'd ever loved him. But that was harsh.

'After the wedding we'll have to find someplace else for this,' she said. 'I won't have it in my marriage bed.'

Simon leant against the apartment door when she reached to unlock it. His expression was cool again, and tired. 'You say that now…' He didn't move, except to gaze down at her chest, and she made a point of folding his money and shoving it into her fake cleavage. They were so close now she could feel his heat through the balloon breasts. Their relationship was like one of those arguments that goes on for ever because neither party will admit defeat. Mercedes unlocked the door and backed away.

When Simon was gone, she shuffled back to the loveseat and slumped down into it, tossing her feet over the side. She ought to shower, but she didn't want to. Would Anwar smell Simon on her? He never had before. Or, if he had, he'd never mentioned it.

Mercedes fished the wad of cash out from between her balloon boobs and shoved it between the couch cushions. She was too exhausted to move, and too aroused to dispose of her humungous breasts. When Anwar arrived, he'd probably laugh, but he'd definitely fuck her without Simon's fuss. God, she needed another go. Spreading her legs, she waited for the door to open.

A Discreet Companion
by Cecilia Duvalle

The first time Nick suggested she hire a gigolo, Karen had laughed and told him to get back to reading his novel. It seemed more than appropriate that he was reading something with colourful art and a fantasy label. The second time it came up was several months later. She was still on top of him, trying to hide her resignation as his come leaked out of her and down around his balls.

'You know, we could get a hired hand in here to toss you on your knees and fuck you crazy,' he said. It was casual and matter-of-fact. His hands cupped her breasts and pulled at her nipples, teasing them into hardness again.

She leant forward and kissed him on the lips.

'No need,' she said. 'I can finish things over here.' She rolled off him, pulled out her vibrator, and brought herself to orgasm in no time while he watched.

The third time, nearly a year after he'd first suggested it, she was on her side, facing away from him. Her fingers were two knuckles deep inside her pussy. She thought he had been asleep for a while, and he startled her when he spoke.

'Hire someone to fuck you the way you want and deserve, please,' he said. 'I want you to have that again, and I can't do it for you.' His soft voice carried no irony, amusement, or anger.

She had rolled back over to face him, her head propped up on her elbow. The moonlight came in through the window and landed on his face in that beautiful blue that made him look like an Adonis. She loved him. How could she have sex with anyone else?

'I'm not unhappy,' she said. 'It's not like I have to have that in my life.'

'Look, I know I can get you off with my mouth, my fingers. All that can work, but I feel that sometimes you just … want a bit more. Even if you ride me until you come, I can never be on top. That old-fashioned he-man style of fucking and pounding your pussy that you can't openly even admit to wanting because you're such a feminist kind of fucking … I know you miss it.'

Just his saying it out loud like that, the words all running together into one long adjective, made her ache for it. Hell, her whole body hungered for the weight of a man on top of her, pushing down against her, and filling her up. She missed the intensity of being physically overwhelmed like that.

She hated him for knowing her so intimately. And loved him for it too.

The fact that Nick couldn't move his lower body had driven him to creative measures in bed. His fingers and hands had found new form, his tongue and lips new motivation. His cock worked, just not his hips or legs. Any fucking relied on Karen being on top doing all the motion. It felt great for him - or so he claimed - and worked for her most of the time. Gone were the days when he could toss her on the bed and fuck her silly. Her favourite position, on her knees with him behind her, his lips and teeth on her neck, was out of the question. They'd managed an approximation with her sitting on him facing away, but it wasn't quite the same as before the accident.

They both knew it.

'You've thought about this a lot, haven't you?'

'Yeah, I have. I want you to do it. And I want to watch.'

'Oh, I see,' Karen laughed. He had always been a bit of a voyeur. She closed her eyes and pictured him sitting next to the bed while another man fucked her, his own hand wrapped around his cock in masturbatory synchronicity.

'OK,' she said, running her finger across his nose and down to his firm but thin lips. 'But I want you to pick him out for me.'

She traced the outline of his mouth in languid orbits until he sucked it in, his tongue swirling around the tip as he licked her finger clean.

'I want you to do the negotiating,' she added for good measure.

'God, you taste good,' he said. 'Let me have more of that.'

She moved to straddle him, grabbed on to the headboard, and ground herself against his mouth until he finished what she hadn't. His lips, tongue, and teeth worked in exquisite rotation until she exploded in orgasm. At the height of it, she pulled herself off his face and plunged his hard cock deep inside her and fucked him hard and fast until she hit a second orgasm, coming just before him. In moments like this, she felt almost completely sated. Almost.

The next morning, after the ritual of getting him up, showered and into his Jazzy Select Ultra, the wheelchair of choice for the lucky and well-to-do, she left him alone so she could hit the gym before work.

He called before lunch.

'You know, you can't just open the phone book and search under gigolo,' he said.

Karen almost jumped out of her chair and looked around her office as if someone might be able to overhear their conversation.

'Phone book? Is that even what they're called? Didn't you look under "male escort" or something like that?' She closed her office door as a precaution.

'Well, that was sort of a joke. "Phone book" and "gigolo" are both things that no one would use any more. But, I'll tell you what, a Google search for "gigolo" doesn't do much either. "*Male companion*" works way better.'

'I can't believe you're doing this,' she said, her voice cracking with the nervous energy of a teenager. 'Just hearing you talk about it sort of makes me horny. And I'm blushing.'

'That's the kind of response I was hoping for,' he said. 'If we're going to blow this kind of money on what amounts to a living blow up toy, I want you to enjoy it. The blushing is just cute.'

'Cute. Great. Nick, you know I could just - find someone to fuck if money is an issue,' she said. Her voice had grown progressively quieter as she spoke to the point she was practically whispering into the phone.

'You mean like go to a bar and just picking someone up?' he asked.

'Yeah, you know, the old-fashioned way,' she said.

'No. That's a problem,' he said.

'Why? It'd be cheaper.'

'True, but it would be complicated. It would be more like a relationship than a business deal. You might get feelings for him. This provides emotional distance.'

'Ah. I see,' she said. He didn't think he would feel jealous if he paid for someone to fuck her? 'Doing it this way means we're really paying for a sophisticated flesh-bot, someone who won't matter beyond his use.'

'Exactly. Someone to entertain you and make you feel good, not make you like him. Think of him as a giant walking, talking dildo. A toy. Something to pleasure you and nothing more.'

'I'd like to think of it as hiring - a discreet companion,' she sad. It sounded a bit more classy than a robotic boy toy. Did he really think she could just fuck someone she had no connection with? She'd never been into one-night stands. Her stomach twisted in knots. It sounded simple on the surface, especially to a man.

'You sound like their websites,' he said, laughing. 'This

isn't exactly as easy as going to a bar. Might take a week or two, or longer. Some of these guys are booked out months ahead. Oh, and honey?'

'Yes?'

'You don't need to whisper. You're not hiding anything from our parents, you know.' She could hear him cracking up as he said goodbye.

In spite of his assurances, she felt weird about it anyway. It wasn't like whoever they found wasn't really a person who had no feelings just because they were a "professional". She was certain some of her friends would completely drop her even though it was Nick's idea to begin with.

She pushed the thoughts aside every time Nick brought up his progress over the next couple of weeks. She would mention a concern, and he'd parry it with a logical rational that she could glomp on to and add to her arsenal to defeat self-doubt. By the time he had found her "perfect man-toy" as he called him, she was actually convinced she was going to be doing something that would not only be fun, but was going to make their marriage stronger and better. It would improve their sex life in the long run.

'Here's his website,' he said one night after declaring the search over.

Karen rested her chin on his shoulder and reached around him to control the mouse. The site was tastefully put together. Brent Carson was clearly fit, knew how to dress, and came across as debonair rather than sleazy in spite of the fact she couldn't see his face in any of the pictures. That made sense. Why show your face to the world when what you did crossed into shady legal boundaries?

Every man they looked at had various versions of the same message. They provided a service that included companionship, conversation, and a romantic time, but sex was not part of the deal. Anything that happened after the official engagement, however, was strictly between two individual adults. They all accepted donations and gifts rather than charged a fee.

'How do you know whether he's going to actually provide sex, or if he really means it that sex is not part of the equation?'

Brent's etiquette page actually said "As I do not offer illegal activities or services, discussing them at any time, through email or in person, will not be tolerated and will be forced to end all future relations".

She didn't want to shell out 1200 bucks and have him just shake her hand at the end of the evening. Now that she was in it, she was really in it for the whole experience. She'd not slept with anyone but Nick for ten years. After talking about it for weeks, she was craving some fresh cock, looking forward to it like she'd been starved of it for years.

'I've had several long telephone calls with him,' Nick said. 'He asked me, in detail, what kinds of things you liked. While I never asked him about having sex with you, I talked about what I used to do with you and what I thought you were missing. He didn't stop me. Just had me talk like he was taking notes. I don't think you need to worry about it, Karen. By the time he's been with you for a couple of hours, he'll be wanting to fuck you, money or no.'

When the date was finally settled, she added it to her calendar. It looked so innocent in black and white. "Dinner with Brent" was all it said. During spare time at work, she kept clicking on his website, looking at the photos of Brent's naked chest, bottom, and sides just like she would if she were buying a new car, constantly checking the specs of the model she'd chosen. She bookmarked the photo of him in his tight black shorts and stole glances at it, imagining her finger running the length of his taut chest straight down to the bulge inside the shorts. She liked what she could see.

She woke up in the middle of the night, slippery wet and in need of sex. Reaching over to Nick, she found him asleep and his cock limp. She woke him up by sucking the whole of him into her mouth, her tongue whirling around the tip,

143

her fingers finding his balls and cupping them gently. She loved the feeling of his cock growing inside her mouth, getting harder and harder until it was too big for her to contain any longer.

'What brought this on?' he asked, his voice drowsy with sleep.

'I'm looking forward to tomorrow night,' she said.

'You mean later tonight,' he said. He reached down to her head and gently pulled on her hair, guiding her up the length of his body. She hovered over him for a moment as he guided her cock into her and she rode him slowly, wanting to keep his pleasure at bay as much as possible.

'I want to be on my knees when he fucks me,' she said.

'Tell me more,' he urged.

'I want him to fuck me hard like that, then I want him to pick me up and toss me onto my back, and ram his cock into me like there's no tomorrow,' she said.

'Damn,' Nick said. 'I'm going to come.'

'You are going to come because you can't wait to watch someone else fuck me,' Karen said, picking up the pace. She tilted her pelvis just right so the head of his cock hit her inside right on her G-spot.

Nick's head arched backward as he fought it.

'No,' he said. 'Going to hold back …'

'Maybe he won't mind if I suck your cock while he fucks me,' she teased. Talking dirty had always been a huge turn-on for her. The words coming out of her mouth fuelled her orgasm just as surely as the feeling of his cock deep inside her.

'I wonder if the two of you can fuck me at the same time,' she said. 'Did you tell Brent that I've wanted that for a long time?'

'Fuck!' Nick exploded inside her.

'Two men at once,' Karen turned four words into a cadence she repeated over and over until she climaxed. 'Two men at once, two … men … at …once …'

She collapsed on top of Nick and fell asleep in his arms.

Nick had Karen dress simply, neither over-the-top sexy or plain Jane. Over a simple lacy bra and panties, she wore a short skirt to show off her long, muscular legs, a lacy camisole and simple jewellery.

The years of dance lessons she and Nick had taken had stuck with her body at least, and she was certain that once on the floor again, she'd have no problem following his lead.

By the time she was dressed, Karen was a nervous, wobbly-kneed, excited wreck. The last time she'd been on a first date had been with Nick. They'd hit it off and she was as good as married. This wasn't exactly a regular date, she knew that, but it was – still - something new.

Nick had arranged for Brent to come to the house, pick up Karen and return her later, but not too late to invite him up for "a drink" after their "official" business was complete. It was hilarious in one sense and nerve-wracking on the other. She fingered the envelope with the "donation" she'd be discreetly handing him soon. Payment in advance. Enough money for her and Nick to fly to Hawaii.

She mixed a couple of martinis and handed one to Nick. She sipped at the other, her stomach flipping hard enough to make the drink sour in her mouth. She put it down and checked that her shoe bag had her suede bottoms in it.

When the doorbell rang, Nick told her to just stay put with her drink and went to the door himself. The low timbre of Brent's voice set her at ease immediately. She had a genuine smile of relief on her face by the time he entered the living room.

He crossed the distance between them in four long strides, took the hand she had offered in his, and lifted it to his lips. She almost laughed it off as fake chivalry, but the sparkle in his eye was too sincere for laughter.

'Karen,' he said. 'It is good to finally meet you. Nick

here has told me so much about you.'

'Apparently so,' Karen said. She knew the kinds of things that Nick had told Brent. That only forced a warm flush across her cheeks.

'He didn't tell me how beautiful you are when you blush, though,' Brent said.

Karen wasn't sure if she liked the smoothness of his compliments. She offered him a drink. He suggested, instead, that they leave right away to make it to the restaurant for the reservations he had made. Nick seconded the motion.

And, like that, Karen realised they were out the door and on their way, leaving Nick behind. She only had a moment to wonder how the envelope she'd put on the coffee table had managed to make it inside Brent's jacket without her even noticing before he helped her into the car.

Dinner was simple and at her favourite Italian place. They never stopped talking, and it was only halfway through the meal that she realised how much Nick had told Brent about her and what she liked. It was as if he'd programmed her date to be just right for her. He wasn't Nick, though. He had his own sense of humour and brought a different kind of warmth to the table. She liked him. Not in a way that could ever conflict with her love for Nick, but she realised before the dessert was served that she could easily have sex with him, enjoy it, and not feel bad about it, especially if Nick was there to cast his approval on the whole scene.

Brent had promised her dancing. She hadn't told Nick just how much she had missed it. It was something that they couldn't even approximate with him in a wheelchair. She felt more like she was about to have an illicit affair when Brent led her onto the floor than if he were leading her to a bed. She cast the thought aside like she had so many before and welcomed his embrace as the rumba got them moving for the evening. She hadn't lost her ability to follow a lead, and soon Brent was changing his frame to bring her closer and closer to him. By the time the first tango played, his hands felt familiar and comfortable against her skin.

Argentinean tango always made her excited, but this one more so. He pulled her into a deep break with her weight on his thigh pressing up into her pussy. With each and every hook, their thighs touched and pressed against each other. When he pulled her into an embracing walk step from behind, his hands moved up to cup her breasts, and his lips brushed her ear.

'Are you ready for me to take you home?' he asked, his breath tickling her in just the right way. He pressed himself against her. The thick bulge of his cock filled the crack her ass with an unspeakable promise.

'Yes,' she said. They finished the tango completely unaware that half the other dancers had stopped to watch them. Nick had always joked that the tango was just the same as having clothed sex on the dance floor.

The ride home was a quiet one. Brent had put his hand on her knee as he pulled out of the parking space and by the time they got back to her house, it was high up her thigh, his finger brushing against the wet cloth of her panties.

He walked her to the door and turned to her with a very serious look on his face.

'Thank you for a lovely evening,' he said. 'I hope you enjoyed my services.'

A jolt of disappointment flooded Karen before she realised what was happening. She recovered quickly and played along.

'Yes. I enjoyed the dinner and the dancing. I understand this concludes the - business portion of the evening,' she said. She shook his hand.

'Perhaps you'd like me to take you dancing again?' he asked.

'Yes. As a matter of fact, I would.'

He turned as if to go, but he seemed to move with a deliberate slowness.

'But, Brent, would you, by any chance, be interested in an after-work night cap?'

She opened the door and he followed her in. Her heart was positively pounding, but not so loudly or fervently as her pussy. She could feel the wetness that had seeped through her panties begin to trickle down her thighs.

She closed the door behind them and grabbed his hand to lead her up to the bedroom. Nick was still in his chair, a book in his hand. He reached around to turn off his reading light when they entered.

'How was the dancing?' he asked.

Brent didn't seem surprised to see Nick in the chair.

'Karen is an amazing dancer,' Brent said. 'She follows a lead like a pro.'

Karen walked across the room and kissed Nick on the lips. He grabbed her hands and kissed them both before releasing them.

Brent stepped up behind close behind her and slid his hands along her rib cage and up her breasts.

'Nick, can I fuck your wife?' he asked casually, as if he made such requests on a daily basis. Maybe he did.

'Please, Brent, fuck my wife like there is no tomorrow.'

Brent backed them away from Nick, not turning Karen around to face him until his calves pressed into the bed. With the same firm lead he would use on the dance floor, he spun her around until they were face to face.

Karen tugged at Brent's tie while he unzipped her skirt. Then they moved with abandon, ripping off each other's clothing as he pulled her into a kiss.

This surprised her. She had thought maybe they wouldn't kiss. It was such an intimate thing to her, even more so than oral or intercourse. But the insistence of his lips and tongue wiped any lingering doubts clear away as efficiently as his hands dealt with her clothing. The next thing she knew, he was lifting her off her feet. She squealed with delight as he tossed her onto her back.

'Oh, you like that, do you?' he asked. He placed his hands on her ankles and ran his hands up her smooth legs to her knees. He parted her legs and knelt between them, his firm body every bit as perfect as his photos. His fully erect cock was thicker but shorter than Nick's and she wanted it inside her.

'I understand you get plenty of oral,' he said. 'But I'd still like to get a taste of you before I fuck you.'

'By all means,' she said.

He kissed her on the lips again and took his time making his way down to her pussy. He nibbled at her neck and lingered at each nipple, ensuring each brown nub was hard and erect. He issued soft kisses along her rib cage and down her belly. By the time his tongue finally found her clit, she was close to coming.

She pushed her hips up toward his mouth, eager for the next step. He licked the juice off her thighs and up her labia to her clit. He flicked his tongue against her with a precision and rapidity that rivalled any of her vibes.

'Oh God,' she said, 'I need you to fuck me.' She put her hands on his head, and tugged at him, pulling him upward. When she could reach his cock, she grabbed his shaft and directed him directly into her waiting, wet hole.

And then he was fully on top of her, a hand on either side of her head, moving in and out of her, pumping his cock into her with abandon.

'Fuck me, oh God, yes.' Her hips thrust upward, meeting each of his thrusts. He pounded into her, giving her what she had been missing.

Just as she started to come, she turned her head and saw Nick pumping away on his cock. Their eyes met as they both exploded in orgasm. It was a promising start to the end of the evening.

Shaming Mrs Sloan
by Alanna Appleton

With a deeply satisfied purr the BMW M3 saloon glided into
a space in the reserved parking area to the rear of the
building. The man who then killed the engine and climbed
from the driving seat to open the rear passenger door wasn't
dressed in any uniform, but he was clearly the chauffeur.
Despite being casually dressed in a black leather jacket, dark
blue open-necked shirt, and faded denims, the deference he
paid to his passenger marked their relationship.

'This shouldn't take too long, I hope,' the woman said.
'Don't wander off, there's a good fellow.'

'I'll resist the urge to wander.' The reply was delivered in
his soft Irish brogue, but in such a dry tone that the
passenger paused a moment, then decided to let it pass.

Her parting glance was disdainful, despite the fact that
Connor Mackie had always been a temptation to her: at six
two he was a couple of inches taller than her, with a
muscular frame and big hands; a short, blunt nose was
entirely suitable for his face, with its deeply dimpled chin
and startling blue eyes.

Turning abruptly, before her interest was noted, Mrs
Evelyn Sloan strode off through the entrance to the parking
area. There was a rear door on the impressive late Victorian
building, but Mrs Sloan never used back doors. In her long-
outdated mindset, they were strictly for deliveries and
servants.

The London street beyond was busy with lunch-time

crowds, and quite a few heads turned for a look at the tall, immaculately dressed woman with the regal posture and impressive frontage who parted the crowds like the prow of a ship parting the ocean swell. She had an unfashionably full figure, with broad hips, rounded buttocks, and proudly jutting breasts that strained the stitching on the varied items of clothing making up an elegantly simple, but very expensive, grey suit. She was in the city on business, and she had dressed appropriately for the occasion. With her flashing green eyes and an upswept mass of auburn hair setting off a classically beautiful, but rather stern-looking face, she reminded some of a 50s movie star. But the full lips were compressed in a line of intolerance for the unwashed crowds she pushed through.

Mrs Sloan was in her early 30s, but had a manner that was usually acquired through decades of subservience from others. She had mastered it early, despite having a near to impoverished upbringing. It was her own drive and talent that had seen her make it to art college and then to a well-paid job with a major clothing label. Marriage to Edward Sloan had been a final step in her meteoric social rise.

Poor Edward! No one had suspected his heart was so weak. True to his independent nature and reserved character, he had told no one.

The well-appointed offices of Berglund and Roth – dark wood panelling and modern art – were as busy as the street outside, with clients seated and awaiting attention, secretaries bustling about with files, phones ringing, and doors opening and closing.

Mrs Sloan had no intention of being seated with the worried-looking supplicants littering the main reception room. She approached an older lady seated in the centre of the storm, looking serene as it all passed over her.

'Miss Greer, I have an appointment at one.' It was said with a glance at her watch, emphasizing the point that 1 o'clock was only a minute off. 'I trust I'm expected.' She gave a pointed glance around the room. 'I have a busy schedule.'

The unmarried and very dedicated Miss Margaret Greer was used to Mrs Sloan's imperious ways and rose from her seat, waving a hand in her easy manner towards the farthest door. 'Mr Berglund is indeed expecting you, and I'm to take you right in.'

She walked Mrs Sloan to the door, rapped briskly once, and then opened it, announcing the arrival of Mr Berglund's very important client.

Henry Berglund was a round, bespectacled little man, with white flyaway wings of hair either side of an otherwise bald pink scalp. He was also respectful, cautious, and exact in his speech. Professional, trustworthy, businesslike, and impersonal – attributes much appreciated by Mrs Sloan. When she needed legal advice, she didn't need any unnecessary personality to come with it.

Today, though, Berglund looked almost nervous!

It was a state Evelyn Sloan would have thought him impervious to. But as he started to speak, his throat went dry and he had to fortify himself by pouring a small measure of brandy from a decanter on his desk. He never kept it there, and he didn't offer any to his client: he knew well that Mrs Sloan would decline.

What on earth could be the matter with the man?

'Apologies,' he said, regaining the use of his voice after a tentative sip at the swirling liquid. 'Went quite dry there for a moment. Now, Mrs Sloan, the matter of your husband's will –' He paused, giving Mrs Sloan a speculative look.

'Yes.' She filled the gap. 'It's about time. You've had a month to sort things out.'

'Well, your husband was a prudent man. We had to track certain monies he'd placed in Jersey and the Isle of Man, and in other more exotic accounts. But we're pleased to inform you that our work in that respect is finished, I hope to your satisfaction once you read the reports. You're financially very well off, Mrs Sloan.' He hesitated once more, removing his spectacles as though not wanting to meet her gaze in any direct way. 'Edward was - an unusual man. No disrespect intended, but his instructions to us were, on occasion, quite outside what might be regarded as - normal. And, of course, you signed a pre-nuptial –'

'I'm quite aware of my husband's nature,' Evelyn snapped. 'But I loved him very much, Mr Berglund, despite his vagaries. I know he was a couple of decades older than me, and I'm sure that fuelled the usual rumours, but I married Edward for love, not gain. If you're about to tell me that he left all his money to the care of traumatised hamsters, that's fine. Just please tell me and I'll be on my way.'

'Well, it's not quite that simple. It is a very large sum of money, Mrs Sloan, and then there's the house, of course. He left Kimbayne House and most of his wealth to you, with certain conditions.'

'Most of it, you say. But he had no other surviving relatives, so who are the other beneficiaries?'

'There is just the one: he left a sizable bequest to his friend and aide, Connor Mackie.'

'Mackie? He's our driver, mechanic, and general dogsbody. Or should I say *my* general dogsbody now that dear Edward is gone.'

'But he and Mr Mackie were very close. It was more like a friendship than an employer/employee relationship, despite a similar age difference to your own. Surely you were aware of that? *I* certainly was. Connor Mackie accompanied your husband on trips to the far corners of the world.'

Mrs Sloan pursed her lips. 'Yes, I thought it entirely inappropriate and told my husband so on many occasions.' She sighed. 'I suppose I'm not surprised he left him something.'

'Well, it's not quite that simple.'

'It's not?'

Mr Berglund fidgeted with some papers in front of him, while Evelyn wondered what on earth was coming. What last folly had Edward left behind?

'I think it's simpler if I just read your late husband's words,' Berglund said. He coughed nervously and began. 'We'll start here – "I have always tried to act in my dear wife's best interests, but loving someone makes it difficult to be firm in correcting their worst character defects. In Evelyn's case I wished to curb the haughty behaviour and delusions of superiority that have grown ever worse during the last few years. Clearly, I failed in exercising the proper discipline that was required. Therefore I bequeath this very difficult task to my much more capable and resourceful friend and confidant, Mr Connor Mackie. I charge him with curbing my wife's unacceptable behaviour, by means that will shame her into an acceptance that humility and charity towards others is required of a person in her position of wealth and influence. This is my last gift to my dear Evelyn." That is all, Mrs Sloan.' Berglund placed the papers on the desk, squaring the edges while his client considered what he'd just read.

During the reading, Evelyn Sloan had been giving him a very direct and disconcerting cold-eyed stare. Now she said, 'What sort of nonsense is this?'

Berglund coughed once more. 'I'm afraid it's your husband's will, legally attested. Mr Mackie has already been informed of his part in it, and accepts his responsibilities. You, Mrs Sloan, are to submit yourself to his discipline or lose your house and money.'

Evelyn's eyes flared angrily. 'Fine. I had a very successful career before I met Edward. I can easily take it up again.'

'In that event, according to your husband's wishes, all assets not bequeathed to Mr Mackie will go to Mrs Marcia Willis.'

'Marcia Willis! Over my dead body!'

'Yes, Edward suggested that would be your reaction. She was your husband's first wife, and I believe there is no love lost between you, am I right?'

'I detest the woman, and I won't have her getting my house. She made it very difficult for me after I married Edward and spread a lot of very hurtful rumours.'

'Indeed, you had to take her to court, as I recall. I represented you myself. I take it then that you do not wish to see Marcia Willis taking possession of Kimbayne House?'

'I would rather die a horrible death.'

For the first time, Henry Berglund permitted himself a tiny smile of satisfaction. 'Fortunately, it won't be quite as bad as that.'

With a sinking feeling in the pit of her stomach, Evelyn knew that Edward had her cornered, and had left her no choice at all. But exactly what he and Connor Mackie had in mind she couldn't guess, although she was sure she wasn't going to like it.

Evelyn avoided either eye contact or conversation with Connor Mackie during the drive back home. Her mind was in turmoil, trying to understand her husband's last mad instructions. The last thing Henry Berglund had handed her was a sealed note from Edward. Opening it she had found only two lines in his untidy handwriting – "I always thought you needed a good spanking, my dear Evelyn, but I was too soft-hearted to give it to you. This is my most important bequest to you, may it do you some good".

Her heart lifted briefly as the car swept through the archway into the inner courtyard. She loved Kimbayne House, a 15th century manor house, ivy-covered and timber-framed, sitting on several hundred acres of landscaped gardens. Dusk was falling and the rows of tall windows reflected the deep indigo of the darkening sky.

Connor opened her door for her, as usual. She walked straight into the house after instructing Connor to put the car in the garage. It was an unnecessary instruction, but she was determined to remind him of his position as a servant. She slipped out of her suit jacket in her favourite room; the lounge with its deep bay widows, high ceiling, comfortable sofas, and wide fireplace. When Connor appeared she demanded he start the evening meal; besides his other talents, Connor Mackie was an excellent chef.

'Not just yet,' he said, in a tone that was much less than deferential.

'I beg your pardon?' She gave him a haughty glare. 'Look, Mr Mackie, whatever freedoms you think my husband gave you, I must caution you –'

'No!' he snapped. 'I must caution *you,* Mrs Sloan. This is exactly the sort of behaviour your late husband has charged me with correcting. I'm forced to concede to his wishes, and I think it best if I make a start with you right now.'

'What on earth are you talking about?'

'A good brisk spanking to start with, Mrs Sloan, the only way Edward believed you could be shamed into some humility.'

'You have to be joking!' Evelyn spluttered, deeply shocked. 'Edward was clearly not in his right mind when he wrote that.'

'You know your husband better than that.' Connor looked around the well-appointed room. 'I think it's entirely too comfortable in here, not the proper ambience at all for a punishment. You'll accompany me into the long hall, if you please.' He walked to the door and looked back. Evelyn hadn't moved.

'I absolutely don't please,' she said.

'Very well, Edward insisted that it has to be with your willing cooperation.' Coming back into the room, he picked up the telephone. 'I'll just tell Henry Berglund that Marcia Willis will be taking possession of Kimbayne House, shall I?'

Evelyn drew in a deep breath. 'You will not.'

'Then you'll accompany me to the long hall?'

'It seems I have no choice.' The words escaped her lips almost as a sigh of despair.

The "long hall", as Edward had liked to call it, was a gallery running most of the length of the north side of the house. Used as a dining hall when they had guests, it had always seemed to Evelyn to be cold and impersonal, even somewhat lonely and forlorn. The long dining table was bare of decoration at the moment, and once Connor had turned on only one of the wall lights, the two rows of empty chairs threw dark shadows along the room. Those chairs seemed somehow possessed of a sinister intent, given what Evelyn now knew she could not avoid. Sure enough, Connor pulled one out and sat himself down.

For a few moments he studied the mistress of the house, and Evelyn felt her pulse quicken. Not for the first time, Connor Mackie's startling blue eyes and roughly handsome face stirred something in her. Something she had always suppressed for love of her husband. Edward had known, though. She was sure of that. Edward had been aware of his wife's hidden desires regarding his closest friend, and in his wise and understanding way, he had neither mentioned it nor resented it.

'Take your clothes off.'

'Excuse me?'

'Strip down to your underwear.' When she didn't move he barked, 'And do it now!'

Evelyn flinched. He'd never been like this with her before. He'd been insolently dismissive of her more imperious commands, and had ignored her frequent slights as though dealing with a temperamental child: something which had always got under her skin. Any complaints about him to her husband had been greeted with an indulgent grin and a complete lack of action. But this was something new. His tone compelled obedience, either that or the thought of losing the house to a hated enemy – or was it more than that?

She felt a thrill of anticipation that should be at odds with her situation.

With his eyes on her, Evelyn Sloan began to undress, dropping her skirt to the floor and unbuttoning her blouse. When she was finally revealed in black heels, black silk underwear, suspender belt, and dark stockings, she saw the look that came over his bluntly handsome face. It was a look of shocked appreciation for the mature, generously curved woman who stood half-naked before him. Somehow the flimsy black silk underwear gave her exposure even more impact than complete nudity might have.

Evelyn shifted uncomfortably under his gaze as it roamed at will over her body: the long, shapely legs, encased in sheer nylon; black knickers moulded to the little mound between her legs; the flat stomach and deeply indented navel, and the full breasts straining against black bra straps. The straps on bra and suspender belt lay snug against soft flesh that glowed in the light of the single lamp. In the cool of the room goosebumps were raised on her thighs and she felt her nipples spring erect in response to the temperature change, aware that Connor could see the coral tips through the dark translucency of the bra cups.

Her feelings were a mixture of embarrassment and gratification as she saw that he was aroused by the sight of her.

He rose and pulled another chair out from under the table, placing the backs of both chairs against one another.

What's he doing? Evelyn wondered. Are we going to sit back to back?

The answer wasn't long in coming. Once Connor had the chairs positioned to his satisfaction, he said, 'Climb up.'

'Pardon?'

'You will climb up on this chair, your back to me.'

'For heaven's sake – why?'

'Just do as you're told.'

Awkwardly, Evelyn placed her knees of the hard surface and shuffled forwards until her bare stomach touched the cold wooden struts of the chair back.

'Now, bend over the back of the chairs and rest your hands on the far seat.'

A shock of humiliation swept through her as she realised the exposure he was about to subject her to. Having no choice in the matter, she leant right over, resting her belly along the top of the chairs and lowering her upper body, somewhat tentatively, down the farthest chair. Her hands grasped the sides of the seat to steady herself.

'This is obscene,' she protested, fully aware of the sight she presented.

Her full, womanly bottom was thrust out, the buttocks spread and rounded, stretching the black silk of her knickers and showing the soft pink flesh as though through a dark, hazy mist. Above the stocking tops her thighs looked softly vulnerable in the light from the single lamp. The black heels added a final touch of incongruity.

'It's going to get even more obscene,' Connor said, 'trust me.'

He placed a splayed hand on her left buttock and she flinched at the feel of his fingers on her sensitive skin. 'Don't move,' he breathed, his voice sounding suddenly ragged with desire. She felt the big hand move across her knickers to the central groove of her bottom and pause.

'I want you right over,' he said harshly. 'Lift your arse up.'

With that, his big blunt fingers were thrust right into her arse crack. Evelyn gasped in humiliated dismay as he said, 'Lift up higher!'

She felt the pressure of his grip on her bottom tighten and fingers pushing on her anus as he urged her further over the chair backs. Only when she was arranged to his satisfaction did he release her.

'I hope you enjoyed that,' she breathed, her cheeks

ablaze with indignation.

He looked around her bent body, at the upturned face glaring back at him, and said, 'I see that made you blush, my lady. Well, let's see how much of a blush I can put on your nether cheeks.'

Without warning, he threw a hard slap across both bottom cheeks, making them pancake and then wobble delightfully. Delightful to Connor, that is, as Evelyn yelped at the sudden assault.

'That hurts!' she gasped.

'That's nothing,' he answered, beginning a barrage of hard smacks across the seat of her flimsy knickers. Evelyn's buttocks jumped and juddered under a series of sharp impacts and her breath escaped in short, shocked exhalations. When he paused at last, he could see the rosy stain on her buttocks through the dark mist of the knickers.

Fighting for breath, Evelyn spluttered out a desperate, 'All right, that's enough! I've taken a spanking, so that's it. Let me up!' She placed her hands flat on the seat and tried to push upwards, but then she felt Connor's hand on her lower back, holding her down.

'Oh no, not by a long shot have you taken your full punishment. That was just intended to warm you up. The real punishment starts now, once I have your knickers down, my lady.'

As his fingers crept under the waistband and pulled on the elastic she cried, 'No! You can't do this! You can't strip me like this! Please!'

'You need to be completely shamed for your behaviour,' Connor told her. 'Both Edward and I agreed on a full spanking punishment, and that means with your arse completely bare.'

The flimsy silk whispered across enflamed skin as he lowered the knickers to her upper thighs. Aware of more movement back there, she asked what he was doing.

'Turning your knickers inside out and draping them

nicely.' He stood back. 'That's quite a picture. How does that feel, my lady? A mature, superior and very haughty woman like yourself, to be bending over those chairs with your knickers down around your thighs and your intimate parts on display – are you feeling properly shamed yet?'

Evelyn didn't answer, but the answer was apparent in the deep red flush on her face.

He can see my bare bottom, my arsehole – her bottom twitched involuntarily, trying to hide the shameful exposure – between my legs – she tried to close her thighs, but her position made it impossible – he can see *everything!*

Then he began to spank her again. The hard smacks, delivered with the full force of his large hand, were even more painful on her naked flesh. Her buttocks churned under the ferocious assault, jumped and juddered as though possessed of independent life, divorced from Evelyn's will as she realised that her frantic gyrations were revealing even more of her intimate parts.

For his part, Connor was enjoying the pink folds of her pussy and the darker skin around her puckered arsehole as her legs and buttocks thrashed about and her heels drummed against the chair seat. Occasionally she tried to push up from the chair, and always he thrust her back down.

He paused a moment to adjust her position as she'd slid back from the highest peak of the chair backs. His method of adjustment was as before, except that her bottom was now naked. His big hand took possession of her bottom as blunt fingers went deep into her arse crack and lifted.

'Oh God! No! Stop it! Stop it! Please!'

But, lying exposed over the chair backs, her buttocks a raw mass of hot agony, Evelyn Sloan didn't mean a word of it. Pain and humiliation had given way to even more shameful enjoyment.

Her attraction to Connor Mackie had always been suppressed, as had her hidden and more primitive desires. Her relationship with Edward had been gentle and civilised, and almost chaste for a married couple, for that was Edward's nature. There had been no roughness or severity in him, and she had often wished there were. How many times had she looked at Connor Mackie and fantasised what it would be like with him?

Well, now she knew.

She sensed the dark enjoyment in him as he stood to one side and resumed his beating of the magnificent bare bottom, so well presented over the backs of the chairs. How long it went on for she couldn't tell. Her buttocks writhed with every hard smack and soon her entire posterior was a deep, angry crimson. Nor did he neglect the soft thigh flesh above her stocking tops. Evelyn gasped and yelped and begged him to stop, but she had already surrendered her bottom to his punishing hand, and no longer tried to rise or resist.

When he finally helped her off the chair, she said in a chastened voice, 'Am I shamed enough?'

He grinned in complete understanding: 'Not quite enough. I think more spankings will be called for. For your sake, I'll stay on here a while and see it done.'

Evelyn couldn't have agreed more.

She stood by Edward's grave the following day and silently thanked him, all the while rubbing at her very sore buttocks.

'You always were attentive to my needs, darling. Your final bequest was much appreciated.'

Myron's Reward
by Cynthia Lucas

It's nice to know that all those years studying at the Royal Conservatory of Music have not been in vain. I sit at my piano bar and warble tunes whose time has come and gone, songs like *Feelings* and *Misty* and, if the customers are in an especially rambunctious mood, *Raindrops Keep Falling on My Head*. I try to smile and act pleasant; I take requests, but I'm more or less ignored. Most of the customers are the after-theatre crowd; some are waiting for their table in the restaurant upstairs so they pop into Moncks's Bar for a drink or two. Sometimes they sit at the piano bar for a listen while talking quietly with one another. My tip jar is a giant brandy snifter and if I'm lucky they will drop a bill or two into it, especially when making requests.

Moncks's is one of those out of the way places, dimly lit with thick plush chairs and candles in little jars on the table. Once in a while the older businessman will come in with a pretty girl on his arm, dripping with diamonds and gold jewellery and I wonder how long she had to blow the old man to get those trinkets. But they're usually good tippers and sometimes the gentleman offers to buy me a drink if I agree to join up with him and his consort when I get off work. I have always declined but lately I'm starting to rethink my options. After all, it's been a long time since I had a good shag. I hope I'm not getting rusty.

But I have other priorities. I only work this shitty job to get enough money for Audrey and Lydia and me to start up our band. It will be a great band, too. We even have a name: The Hot Pussies, featuring me, Barb Wheeler, on piano and vocals. We'll play real music – good old-fashioned rock and roll, the kind that seems to have been forgotten in this day of hip hop and gangsta rap, the kind with a good beat, the kind of music people can dance to. It's the music I grew up on and it's the only kind that resonates with my soul.

Gordy Moncks owns the bar. He's a squat, balding old fart with liver spots on his pate. He reeks of cheap cologne and wears suits too tight and gold chains round his neck and wrists. I know he only hired me because he likes to ogle my cleavage and slap my ass whenever he gets the chance. He thinks he might have a chance with me because I wear clingy dresses with plunging necklines. My favourite is a tight leather gown that drops down just below the knees and has teardrop-shaped holes cut out in all the right places. It's good for business. If I wear that dress I know I can clear at least a hundred in tips that night.

From my place at the piano I have a clear view of the bar, a grand old structure of dark mahogany and polished brass fixtures and twinkling liquor bottles on glass shelves behind it. Gordy's son, Myron, mans the bar. He's not much better-looking than his father, a thin, mousy young man in heavy horn-rimmed glasses and cheap, ill-fitting suits. If there ever was a definition for "nerd", Myron would be it. Unlike his father, he's pleasant enough and often flashes me a smile and a thumbs-up when business is going well. I wink back at him, just to be nice, and his pussy-tickler moustache lifts under his smile.

But it's three in the morning and I'm getting hoarse. The waitresses are collecting dirty glasses and lifting the chairs upside down on the tables for the cleaning crew to come through later in the morning. The last of the patrons stagger out on wobbly legs and hail taxis on the kerb. It's raining tonight and I don't relish the long walk to the bus stop. I would call a cab for myself but I can't afford it. I have to scrimp every last cent I can if I want to get out of this lousy job.

I cover the piano with a black velvet cloth, gather my tips, and saunter up to the bar where Myron stands polishing the last of the glasses. Though he looks tired, there's a mischievous gleam in his eyes.

'Long night, Barb?' he asks as he pours me a Chivas. I'm entitled to one free drink after my shift.

'Longer than I like,' I reply. The liquor burns my scratchy throat but it feels good, almost sensual. 'But I won't be here for long.'

'Oh?' Myron lifts one eyebrow as he stuffs a clean cloth into a glass and twists.

'I'm just here to make some money so I can start a band with my girlfriends,' I say and push my empty glass toward him. He pours me another, one I will have to pay for myself. But to hell with it. I'll use the money from my tip jar.

'What kind of band?' he asks.

Before I know it, I'm pouring my heart out to this timid little geek, telling him all about my band, the music we'll play, the cities we'll tour, the fame, the money, the glory. All we need a little bit more cash to get started. We're almost there. We just need a few more weeks and soon we'll have enough for new amps and Lydia's guitar. We even have our first gig lined up at a club in Soho. After that, we'll be rich and famous and I can kiss old man Moncks's ass goodbye. I'll never have to beg for cock again.

'Sounds pretty ambitious,' Myron says when I finish.

'You don't get anywhere in life without ambition,' I reply. 'You have to take chances.'

Myron nods. 'You're absolutely right.'

I finish my drink and head out through the kitchen where the lone cook is polishing the last of the hors d'oeuvre dishes. There is a small room adjacent to it, little more than a broom closet, that serves as my dressing room. I have a small vanity table with a mirror where I can check my make-up and a rack where I keep my dresses. A narrow, threadbare couch is up against the far wall where I sometime doze between sets. It's cramped and stuffy in there; I feel sorry for the poor sap Mr Moncks will hire to replace me.

I turn around and notice that Myron has followed me in. He's visibly nervous. His hands tremble as he closes the door behind him.

'What do you want?' I ask.

Myron's eyes dart across the room as though he's surveying all my personal things. He clears his throat and nervously says, 'Want to make some money?'

I immediately grow suspicious. 'How?'

'You could do some favours for me.' Myron digs into his pocket and pulls out a thick wad of cash that he fans out like a deck of cards. They're not just dollar bills. There's tens, twenties, fifties, even a few hundreds. I have no idea how he came across that much money.

'What kind of favours?' I demand.

Myron hands me a $50 bill and stuffs the rest of the wad back into his pocket.

'I'll give you $50 if you let me look at your tits.'

My first instinct is to throw the money back at Myron and flee the dressing room. How dare he? Mr Moncks should know what kind of perverse little horny toad he's spawned. I crumple the bill in my hand and prepare to launch it at Myron but I suddenly stop, intrigued. It's been a long time since I felt something that big in my hand. Besides, he only wants to look at my tits. Can you blame him? If I do say so myself, I've got a nice, voluptuous rack that would put Marilyn Monroe herself to shame. And it's been way too long since any man has seen it.

'OK,' I agree. 'But just for a few minutes.'

Myron readily agrees with a few quick nods of his head and starts rubbing his hands together in anticipation. I let the straps of my gown slip down my shoulders. My creamy, magnificent globes pop out from the top of the bodice. The nipples are pink and pliant as bubble gum and hard and erect.

Myron gazes at them with the wonder of a pilgrim beholding a miracle. He leans closer, sighing so I can feel his warm breath caress the flesh and raise the nipples ever higher. I must admit, I find it divinely sensual. I lean up to him so he can get the full view, cupping my tits in both hands.

'They're beautiful!' he sighs and reaches out to them. I pull back and he stops short. 'Can I touch them?'

'Only for another 50 bucks,' I say.

Myron digs into his pocket and gleefully pulls out the cash. He caresses my breasts, gingerly at first, then works up to a stronger touch, pinching my nipples and rolling them between his thumb and finger. I moan and lean into his hands. Sparks I had thought were long extinguish zip down my body, spreading delightful warmth deep inside my pussy. Myron is moaning too, his eyes never leaving those magnificent globes. He leans closer until his lips barely touch the hard, rubbery nubs of my nipples.

'Can I suck them?' he begs.

'It'll cost you another hundred.'

Myron hands me the money and his warm, dewy mouth kisses the pale flesh around one nipple then the other. He's grunting softly as he cups his mouth over the nipple. His tongue and lips send spasms of pleasure coursing through me. He sucks hard, caressing one breast before moving onto the other. His moustache tickles and raises gooseflesh over my entire body. I start to wonder what else that little moustache can tickle.

'You're beautiful!' he sighs between groans. 'Oh God! I want you all. Take off the dress.'

I reluctantly pull back. By now my pussy is throbbing and my nerves are jangling for more. My tits are gleaming from his mouth and I smoothly rub my hands across them.

'If you want to see it all it will cost you another 200,' I

say.

Myron doesn't hesitate in handing over the money. By now I can see his cock tenting the cheap polyester fabric of his trousers. I want to reach out and grab it but I hold back. If he wants that, he'll have to pay.

I shimmy out of my dress and let it fall in a blue sequined puddle at my feet. I'm wearing a skimpy thong panty that just barely covers my shaved snatch. Myron gasps when he sees me and plunges back into my breasts, licking, sucking, pinching the nipples and snagging them between his teeth. A bolt of pleasure races through me and my legs buckle. I collapse on the narrow couch and arch my back against Myron's touch. Instinctively, I spread my knees and Myron nestles between them. I want it all and I want it now. I don't know how much longer I can hold off. The tip of his cock rubs against my clit, safely encased in my panties. I try to hold back but I can't help bucking against it.

'Take off the panties.' Myron sits up and loosens his belt. The pants slide down his hips and there is a little wet spot on the front of his polka dotted boxer shorts.

I hold up three trembling fingers. 'Three hundred.'

Myron places the bills on the vanity table and I hook my thumb through a thong and pull my panties off, letting them fall wherever they may. Myron separates my knees and gazes gratefully at my glistening, exposed snatch. I trail a finger across the slit and suck off the tasty juice.

'Oh, my God!' Myron gasps as though he's never seen a pussy before. He keeps moaning, 'Oh! Oh! Oh!'

Without even asking, he throws $500 on the vanity and plunges his face between my thighs. The shock of the sensation throws me off guard. I arch my back and groan, bucking my cunt against that expert tongue. I was right. That moustache tickles my clit in a heavenly way as he works his tongue along my steaming slit, all the way down into my asshole and starts rimming me for all he's worth. I want to come. God, how badly I want to come! But I must hold back. Myron has to pay for that.

When he pulls away his face is gleaming and the moustache is beaded with my succulent juice. Somehow he has worked his way out of his boxers and his rigid dick stands thick and mighty. I never would have guessed that such a geeky little runt would have such a tremendous cock. It's hard and meaty, a good ten inches with a big, flared head dripping with dew. I reach out and stroke it, moistening the head with my tongue. This one is free, but I still hear the rustle of bills as Myron drops them on the table.

He rubs his fingers through my hair and whispers, 'Do you like to fuck?'

I nod eagerly and lean back against the cushions on the couch. He towers over me and rams that magnificent cock deep into my throbbing cunt. I arch my back and cry out. The pleasure is so intense I can't hold back any longer. Wave after wave washes over me as he thrusts and pounds, deeper and harder, until I feel my orgasm explode throughout my body.

'Play with your tits!' he commands and I obediently comply, kneading the velvety flesh and rolling my nipples between my fingers.

Myron groans as he comes, pulling his dick out of my twat and splattering my belly with hot creamy jism. I gather it up and suck it from my fingers. It's hot and salty and oh so delicious.

'Mmmmm ...' I sigh as I smear whatever is left across my tits.

Panting, Myron collapses on top of me, his heart beating rapidly against mine. His moustache tickles as I plant a long, slow kiss upon his lips. I never realised how sensuous they are – firm and fleshy and soft as iris petals. He may be a nerd but I think I can spend a lot more time with this man.

We hear footfalls just outside the door. It must be old man Moncks making his final rounds through the bar before closing up for the night. We dress hurriedly before he has a chance to knock on the door and walk right in. Myron drops the last of his cash on the pile by the couch.

'Here,' he says. 'Take it. It's all I have but you're worth it.'

I count the money. There's $2000 all together.

'I can't take all this,' I say and try to hand it back to him. He pushes it back.

'Keep it,' he says. 'I have plenty more and you need the money more than I do.'

I tuck the money into my purse just as Mr Moncks bangs on the door.

'What's going on in there?' he demands.

I open the door. Mr Moncks's bulbous head is red with rising fury when he sees Myron and me standing there. I smile and look him directly in the eye. I can finally say the words I've been longing to tell him for months.

'I quit!'

And I leave.

The Third Party
by Sommer Marsden

'You can't be serious.' I stared at Gil and he looked as serious as a heart attack. A handsome one, but still a heart attack.

'I think it would work. If we do it about three times we have enough for that balloon payment.'

'That's $30,000,' I breathed.

'And would save our house.'

'But ... still ...' I wasn't saying no but fear beat a steady thick pulse in my temples.

'Ten grand per visit, three visits. *Three*, Vivian. Less than an hour each. And no one – no one touches you but me.'

The thought of that room – that room full of strangers, staring. Watching. Doing God knows what to the sight of us together. It made me feel dizzy. But under it, if I paused to look, I noticed a thin and frilly ripple of excitement too.

'How?' I started and my husband startled me by kissing me. His big hands clamped to my hips, his mouth rough and bullying. A surge of wetness started in my pussy, my sex suddenly slick inside my panties.

I tried to catch my breath when he pulled back. He answered my unfinished question.

'That place, Holly-weird. We went there –'

'For Nick's bachelor party.'

'Right.' His eyes were on me, bright and curious. He was studying me and it made me hot and prickly all over.

'And?'

He shrugged, his cheeks colouring, but his eyes never leaving me. 'It's a variety. There are dancing booths. You can watch the girls dance for ten. Watch them ….' He cleared his throat and I waited. Holding my breath. Heart pounding.

'Watch them what?'

Big brown eyes flashed with a trace of guilt but then he smiled. 'You can watch them get off for 20. You can watch them with a guy for 50. And …'

'And?'

'And you can get the partition to rise for 200. Ten minutes.'

I swallowed hard. 'Did you get the partition to rise, Gil?'

He shook his head and looked chagrined. 'Nope. I'm a pussy. I only watched her get off. Alone.'

Anger rippled under my skin, but right on its tail, chasing it along, was a trail of arousal I'd never admit to. Ever.

'I see.'

'Don't be mad. It's no worse than watching porn. The thought of how bad it is makes it so good. And then I came home and fucked my pretty wife.'

He reached out to pinch my hard nipples. They pressed traitorously against my navy blue pullover. Maybe I didn't *need* to admit to my sinister arousal. I cleared my throat and tried to think beyond the wet pounding in my cunt.

'And how did this happen?' I asked.

'Howard was talking to the guy who runs the sex show …' He blushed when he said it as if he hadn't just suggested we perform in said sex show to save our home.

'And?' I was getting annoyed. But still, under all of it, a slow and steady hum of excitement. Like electricity running through water.

'Howard said, "Show the guy your wife." I showed him your picture. He asked me if it was current.'

I gaped at him. 'Why?'

'I guess to see if it was old and maybe you'd had a dozen

172

or so kids since then.' Gil shrugged. 'I don't know, babe.'
He reached out boldly and cupped my mound through my
yoga pants.

I didn't make him move his hand.

'And then he looked me over and said the third Thursday
of every month was live sex night. Pretty couples
performed. People watched. People – did other things. They
paid a hefty overhead and the club is shut down but for those
attending and it appears dark from the outside to prevent
raids and yada, yada, yada…'

'Yada, yada, yada!' I squeaked. 'This is sex for money.
In front of people. For money!'

'You said that.'

'It bears saying twice.'

'I know,' he said. His arm, as big as my thigh and
muscular, snaked around my waist and pulled me in. Gil
didn't tower over me, but he was huge. I was five foot ten,
he was six three. He made me feel small sometimes. Which
was a feat.

'I mean … Could we?'

'You want to,' he said, kissing down my throat.

Invisible icy fingers slid down my skin with his kiss. My
arms erupted in goosebumps and I shivered, my pussy
flexing wetly against nothing. I wanted him in me – moving
and filling me. I wanted it now and I didn't want to wait.
But I stayed silent.

'Why do you say that?' My voice was a gasp.

Gil pulled back and cupped my face in his hands. He
stared into my eyes even as he leant in to press his pelvis to
mine. The length of his hard-on kissed the split of my nether
lips. I wanted so badly for my pants to be gone.

'I can see it in those big blue eyes, pretty wife. The
moment I brought it up there was interest. Your pupils
dilated and your cheeks turned pink. You licked your lips.
You started breathing heavy …'

All of this monologue was punctuated by intense

sweeping motions of his thumbs over my nipples. I writhed in his embrace, unable to stay completely still as he talked to me, touched me.

'Did I?'

'Yes.' Gil unzipped my sweater and pulled the cups of my bra down. His mouth was searing and demanding as he licked and bit my nipples until I was wrestling with his belt.

'You want people to watch us fuck,' he said, mouth pressed to my ear. The heat of his breath warmed me, and I sighed aloud. I finally got my hand in his pants, his cock in my grip.

Gil tugged down my yoga pants and pushed me to the kitchen table.

'What are we doing?' I asked softly as he pressed his wet mouth to my wetter pussy. He licked me until I came with a long, low moan. It was only when he had his cock in hand and was parting my thighs that he answered.

'This is dress rehearsal.'

It wasn't what I meant, but at that point, the question wasn't important any more.

'I'm going to pass out,' I whispered.

'You aren't going to pass out.'

'I'm going to.' I sighed.

'No you won't. Just focus, baby. It's me and you. No different than any night we've ever been together.'

'Barring all the people watching,' I gasped, and he squeezed my hand.

'Right,' Gil said.

'And masturbating, probably,' I whispered.

'Almost definitely,' he said.

How they could all sit around and jerk off or rub one out as others pressed close and watched too was beyond me. But then again, it wasn't. Because when I let myself think it and explore it in my mind, I grew flushed. Some of my nerves passed. My belly unclenched and terror was replaced with anticipation.

'I am a pervert,' I said.

He barked out laughter. 'Why? You starting to get into this, Viv?'

I nodded and put his hand over my jumping breast. My heart pounded raucously beneath the flesh. 'God help me, I think I am.'

'Good. Because it's getting me off a little too,' he whispered right in my ear so I could hear him above the general din of the large club. It was packed out there; we could hear the bustle and shift of a large room full of people.

Waiting.

To watch us fuck.

'We'll do fine. If we hate it, we don't have to do it any more,' I said.

'Right.' His hand probed beneath the short silk flowered robe they'd given me. Under it, I was bare. As instructed. Gil parted my pussy lips with his thick fingers, drove into me swiftly.

'But I doubt that not liking it will be a problem. And honestly …'

'Honestly, what?' I asked as the curtain started to part and light flooded my vision.

'Honestly, my worry is about lasting now. I'm so worked up to fuck you in front of a room full of strangers I think I might come right now.'

'You'll last,' I said.

A thin Asian man with the androgynous face of a rock star waved us through. We went and I said, 'I'm the lucky one.'

'What do you mean?'

'I get to come as many times as I want. They encourage that,' I whispered.

'Lucky girl.'

We walked up the centre aisle as we'd been told and

though I tried so hard to look left or right, the overhead track lighting was set to the "surface of the sun" setting and I couldn't see anything beyond the white-carpeted floor we travelled. Here and there were the edges of the chair legs, like black fingers pressing the white trail under my feet.

At the last moment, I turned fast – bold and unthinking – and faced the crowd. I blinked in the lights, Gil's hands pulling at me to come with him. At first I was confused and then it hit me and a fresh sizzle of excitement snaked through the core of me.

'Come on, Viv.

I went. As we climbed the steps, I whispered to him, 'Masks.'

He squeezed my hand. 'What?'

'They're all wearing masks.'

It made sense. They were watching strangers fuck. Paying big money to watch it live in an exclusive club that had been shut down for just this purpose. Part of the draw was our normalcy – me and my Gil. We weren't pros or porn stars. We were simply people fucking on stage for money. To a lot, that was taboo. And to many, as was evidenced here, that was a huge turn-on.

Masks. They were all wearing masks. Strangers watching him take me. Sitting shoulder to shoulder. Touching themselves. Jacking off … Coming in public.

I moaned and we both stilled to hear it. Gil touched my face. 'We're here.'

'We are.' My pulse was thundering between my legs and he could feel it. He could hear it and see it. We'd been together too long for him not to read me like a book.

He dropped to his knees and I realised that in this insanely bright light it was as if we were alone. We couldn't really see or even hear the other people. A hush was in the room and the track lighting that served as spotlights blotted out all the world. But for Gil.

It was only the energy of the others that I could pick up

on. It licked along my flanks and over my back like ghost fingers. The air hummed with the gathered presence of bodies. Silent, attentive, *masked* faces.

When my husband pressed his face to my pussy, with only the tissue thin silk of my robe separating us – and nothing else – I damn near came.

He turned me and I let him. Gil was one for a heavy dose of pre-sex ass worship. His mouth tender and humbling on the small of my back, the slope of my ass cheeks. He kissed the right one thoroughly before biting me hard enough to make me jump – to make me even wetter – and then he moved to my left side. His hand came up between my legs and he touched me. Just my clit at first. Most likely his hand was obscured by my robe; I hadn't removed it yet. But when I gasped, there was an echoing gasp in the audience that set my skin to tingling.

His tongue trailed down the crack of my ass, his fingers buried in me to the hilt. He was fucking me with his fingers and even I could hear the wet sounds of my sex accepting him. Even above the pounding of my heart in my ears.

A rustling of fabric … A sigh of skin on skin … What sounded like someone kissing. These were the sounds that travelled to me. A tiny gasp was heard as Gil curled his fingers. The gasp did me in. It was not my gasp. It was the sound of someone else enjoying what they were seeing. Our sex. Our coupling. Our need. Naked and brushed in bright yellow spotlight on a clinical, cool stage.

I opened my robe and let it drop.

He turned me, almost like he was displaying me. I went in slow motion like a lethargic ballerina in the spotlight. I expected to feel self-conscious. To be worried about how my body looked. Instead, I felt the warm kiss of the bright lights on my skin. And the bated breath of everyone watching us. The warm, wet drag of Gil's tongue on my clitoris and the probing, rigid length of his fingers in my cunt. At any moment I might come again. The drum beat of my heart and the weakness in my knees told me so.

'Part your legs.' His words were no more than a puff of air on my skin but I heard him somehow. I heard him clearly and took a step out so that my body was more open to him. Gil shuffled closer on his knees, still clothed in just the pinstriped black trousers they'd given him. But he'd pulled his cock free and was jerking his erection with an aggressive hand. I hummed softly, loving the sight of his hand on his dick, and buried my fingers in his dark brown hair. I held him to me as he licked me, eating me out so thoroughly I felt a little light-headed with it. I almost forgot them all out there and yet, when someone cleared their throat in the audience, the image of them roared in my head. A sea of strangers wearing masks. Watching us. Touching us without touching us as we were intimate – with their eyes and their energy.

I came again. A warm rush of fluid sliding free of me.

That was when Gil growled roughly, took my hands and pulled me down. He flipped me to my hands and knees; the cuddle-soft fabric of my discarded robe rested under my left hand. I curled my fingers in it, dropped my head and heard my hair slide along the stark white carpet.

'I'm sorry to be such an animal,' he said, his teeth on my earlobe as he brushed his hands along my skin. My neck, my shoulders, down my arms so I shivered. He smoothed his palms along the length of my back and palmed my ass, before leaning in to say, 'I promise I will fuck you nice and slow and face to face at home. I will lavish you with attention and treat you like the perfect woman you are. But this – this is doing strange things to me. I just want to –'

'Gil?' I gasped, turning my head to kiss him briefly.

'What?'

'Shut up and fuck me.'

That was that. He mounted me, very much in the way of the animal he compared himself to. His cock speared me, impaled me, parted and filled me, and I moaned, forcing myself back to aid him. I gripped the carpet as my body adjusted, but then bucked wildly when he surprised me by pushing his finger into my ass.

Someone in the audience sighed and I pinched my nipple hard, the sound and the feeling equally shocking. My internal muscles grew rigid, clamped down on Gil's thrusting cock, and he gripped me so hard at the hips I wondered about fingerprints. Lasting for days. Dark eggplant marks that proved I was his.

A ripple sounded deep inside me and I knew that I had at least one more release coming my way. I could feel it rushing toward me like a summer storm. He added a second finger to the one already thrusting into my ass and I cried out. There was an answering cry. One that sounded very much like an orgasmic release.

I heard Gil say, 'Jesus,' and knew he was just hanging on. Any false move on my part could put us at the end. The only thing we needed to do – beyond fuck – was last as long as possible.

He pulled free of me and his absence was staggering. My skin was hot from the lights and the adrenaline. My muscles blazing from our movements. Gil stood and I stayed put on hands and knees like a good little girl. When his cock pressed to my lower lip, I opened my mouth for him. Stuck out my tongue and licked him. Drew on him with a long, lazy suck as someone in the invisible throng grunted.

Gil buried his hands in my hair and tugged enough to make my lips go rigid on his erection. I hissed a little and then sucked him harder, letting him drive into my mouth with force. Making me gag. Running my eye make-up for all our admirers to see.

I touched myself more for me than for them, but I heard the appreciative sounds of the watchers. It occurred to me as I plucked and pinched my clit to a rigid little knot that the only thing *not* running through my head was the money. The money was what had brought us here, but had been the only thing absent from my thoughts.

'Sorry,' he growled and dropped to his knees. Gil moved around behind me again, driving into me so easily. Aided by the slippery lube of my saliva on his hard-on. The break had only served to make my pussy plumper and more sensitive. Every slide of his sex into mine was a blissful kiss. Every bit of friction, a godsend.

I put my head down, chanting, 'Yes, yes, yes ...,' as if we were the only ones here. To me we were. None of them mattered. The unseen bright light viewers who were touching themselves or each other or just storing all this for later when they could do just that. It didn't matter. All that mattered was how good it felt, how much I loved him ... God, how much I trusted him.

His finger breached my ass again and that bite of pain did me in. 'Baby,' I sighed and I was coming. Sobbing. Making it big and loud and unmistakable. But more for him than for them.

Gil drove deep once, twice, three times before pulling free of me. The emptiness was staggering when it happened. But then I felt the searing baptism of his come on my lower back. Patterns of fluid on my skin that, in my mind, were luminescent. Glowing like deep sea creatures in the blackest waters.

He leant over me, wrapping his arms around my middle. We had been instructed to stay here. On the stage. Not to move or leave. They would keep the lights up and clear the room before alerting us.

So we stayed.

'You think you can do this a few more times? To save the house? To get everything in order?'

I thought of the sex we'd just had. What felt very much like a threeway, but much safer to my heart. Me, him and the third party – an unseen, unheard, voracious sea of watchers who did not touch or penetrate or ... matter. The thrill of it had been eye-opening. My acceptance of it both amusing and bizarre.

'Truth be told,' I said, sitting up and turning to him. I kept my voice to a whisper, I did not know if anyone was listening. I did not know if we were alone. 'I could get rich doing this. I could see me craving this, Gil.'

Gil smiled. 'God, I love you. You are so dirty.'

Apparently, I was.

Black Swan
by Scarlett Blue

Men think strippers are all sex-crazed bisexuals, and to be fair, we do nothing to dispel this myth, as a lot of money can come from a bit of well-placed lipstick lesbianism, but we're rarely really into it. It's a rare woman who takes my eye; I like the hardness of men's bodies, that manly smell, the way a man can dominate me physically. I love showing off my body, so I enjoy giving lap dances, knowing that they desire me, and will wank over me later, or think about me when they're fucking their wife. But so many customers are submissive, and that's such a turn-off for me; I'm a submissive through and through. This sometimes surprises people as I'm confident and assertive, and often wear the trousers in relationships, but I tend to subscribe to the theory that people are the opposite in bed to how they are in life. I often smirk to myself when I see couples who have a certain power dynamic in the street, as I always imagine it's reversed in the bedroom.

For some reason I was thinking about this last night as I was dancing for a nondescript customer, holding faux-intense eye contact as I slid my thong over my hips and watched his eyes dart to my bare pussy and back to my eyes. That familiar submissive look they get in their eyes, it's so boring to me; I like a man who will grab me by the hair and tell me what to do, and has the physical power to back it up. That's why I'm into men, I've always struggled to imagine a woman could overpower me like that. Until last night, anyway.

I finished up with the customer, and after I'd rejected his requests to meet him at a hotel later and "make him my slave" he wandered off, adjusting his erection through his suit trousers. If only he knew that all he had to do to get me home was *tell* me I was going home with him and that he was going to fuck me however he wanted, instead of meekly asking for the honour of my company …

I dressed and walked downstairs into the main club, where girls danced and stripped naked on stage and mingled with the customers, trying to get them upstairs for a private dance, where the real money changed hands. I leant on the bar, surreptitiously counting my money inside my sparkly evening purse and scanning the bar for anyone who might be eyeing me up and looking desperate, drunk, or rich enough to part with some cash. The usual bleached blonde cardboard cut-out was dancing on stage, attracting a vague interest from the men around the stage as her top came off, and more as her knickers came down, as they strained for a look at her pussy as she paraded round the pole.

I used to fantasise when I was on that raised stage that the men would all close in on me, start telling me what to do, start pulling off my underwear, telling me to open my legs, bend over, lie down, loads of them watching me, shouting out orders, calling me a filthy bitch when I carried them all out without argument. I'd end up on my back with my legs over my shoulders, rubbing my wet pussy. Before my fantasy reached its dénouement of men taking it in turns to lick my pussy and being fucked on stage in front of everyone, I was pulled out of my reverie by a furore near the stage. Some new girls were auditioning. They do auditions while the club's open to make sure the girls can actually cope with an audience. New faces are always popular with the customers – men's appetite for a pussy they've never seen before is never satiated – and the girls like to watch them to check out the competition, and have a snide snigger at those shy young ones who can't do pole tricks, and look genuinely embarrassed getting their tits and pussies out in public.

The first one up was one of these. She looked about 19, had highlighted blonde hair and was wearing a sort of prom dress and satin high-heeled sandals. She was hot, but didn't look like a stripper at all. She was dancing to a Britney song, and started to gyrate as every eye in the house was on her. Her cheeks flushed as she struggled out of the dress. Proper exotic dancer clothes slip on and off easily, and those ubiquitous PVC platform shoes are actually really comfortable and well-balanced, but it takes newbies a while to figure this out, and everyone starts out struggling to do a slick striptease in normal underwear and shoes. She danced self-consciously in her underwear, and I saw the manager in the DJ booth signalling her to take them off. She was bright red as her bra came off, to a murmur of appreciation from the men, as her perky young breasts dominated the room. She ran her hands over them, her clumsy movements and lack of ability to pilot her own desirability reminding me of my own entrance to the sex industry years earlier. The men were starting to gather closer in anticipation of her pussy being on show, and her hands were trembling as she gripped the sides of her white lacy knickers. She pressed her back into the pole and I saw her visibly take a deep breath before she pulled her knickers down. There was a faint ripple of applause and the sexual energy in the room increased. She tried to cover herself with her hand, but the manager signalled to her to move her hand, and her legs were clamped together, almost crossed, as she ran her hands up her naked body. I knew she'd get the job just on being young and attractive even though her dancing left a lot to be desired. While many customers like the hardened professional, for many that hint of shame was part of the appeal. My imagination took over where her lacklustre but still strangely sexy performance ended, as in my head the men stormed the stage, forced her to open her legs and finger-fucked her, and she loved every second of it. One day I wanted to open my own strip club, free of all these rules and limitations, where the girls really were filthy nymphos, and the men wanted to have their way with them.

I was in such a horny mood, I really needed to find another customer so I could get him upstairs and at least masturbate while he watched, and disappear into my fantasy world where he would force me onto my knees and make me crawl around naked, instead of staring blankly at me, overwhelmed. There wasn't much point trying to score a customer while the auditions were going on, though, so I ordered a glass of wine and took a seat by the stage to watch the show. After two more embarrassed teenagers that I have to admit made my pussy wet with their shyness, the next girl really caught my eye. She was dressed in a fetishy strappy black bodysuit, thick white shiny tights and black leather pointe shoes, laced tight and symmetrical up her legs. The manager and DJ were exchanging quizzical glances, the customers were staring with that panicked look men get when they're aroused but don't know how to handle something, and the neon bikini-clad dancers were sniggering behind their acrylic nail tips. Stripper fashions don't change much over the years, and the one thing that is absolutely set in stone is high-heeled shoes. It was the flouting of this unspoken rule that had piqued everyone's interest, and how the hell she was going to strip wearing tights I had no idea!

The music – not your usual coquettish cheesecake pop, but a heavy, creepy, industrial track – started, and she began to dance. Her body arched and she snapped up on pointe, lifting one foot and effortlessly touching it to the back of her head. She released the foot and slid down into the splits, her chest and head dropping onto her front leg easily. I couldn't take my eyes off her. There was something indecent, and beautiful, about the curve of her foot in those shoes. She rolled towards the pole and grasped it against her shoulder, swinging her body into the air and maintaining the split. Her small, round breasts peeped over the top of her costume as she did so. There was something hot about a flash that was – or seemed – accidental, compared to the bored, practised way many experienced strippers took their clothes off. She scaled the pole with no problem at all, no mean feat, especially wearing tights which gave no grip against the legs. She flipped upside down and her breasts were fully exposed. When she reached the floor she landed in a perfect pointe, and ripped the front of her costume down, dropping the bodysuit to the floor and stepping out of it. She had an incredible slim, toned figure and very pale skin which was dramatic against her black hair. While the effect of being topless in the tights was weird, the difference made it incredibly sexy. I was transfixed by her elegance and strength, but still interested to see how she was going to strip naked with the pointe shoes on over the tights. The manager was keeping a close eye on the customers' reactions, who were all as entranced as I was. The girl slinked to the floor again and reclined on her back, opening her legs wide, her feet still arched in the bondage of the pointe shoes. She ran her hands down the inside of her thighs, took hold of the shiny Lycra in her fingers and ripped a rough hole in the crotch of the tights. She wasn't wearing anything underneath, and the sudden sight of her juicy, spread open pink pussy against the untainted white fabric was shocking.

My pussy was throbbing insistently, demanding I get to know this girl. Despite having totally confused everyone, she'd also turned them all on so it was obvious she'd got the job, so I followed her to the changing rooms. I started touching up my make-up and watched in the mirror as she carefully unlaced the pointe shoes and stripped off the destroyed tights, replacing them with a black rubber minidress. She produced another pair of pointe shoes, this time not the traditional ballet kind, but the made-for-fetish shiny black ones, with spike heels that forced the wearer into a permanent pointe. I was openly staring and she addressed me sharply, in perfect English but with more than a hint of a Russian or Eastern European accent.

'Would you like to try them on?'

She didn't have to ask me twice. I kicked off my high mules and sat on the make-up counter as she took hold of my foot, cradling the arch in her hands, smoothing out my stocking with a touch somewhere between tender and impersonal, like someone dusting an expensive inanimate object. She seemed to decide the shoes would be better without the stockings and moved up my leg to unclip them, but I was wearing a one-piece garter belt and stockings that didn't unclip, with my thong over the top, in order to give my customers a sexy view of my naked pussy framed by the stockings and suspenders.

'You'll have to take them off,' she said. Not that I would have protested, but before I had the chance she guided me backwards and peeled off my knickers and stockings in one go, stretching the stockings out as they slid over my feet, letting the slightly cold air kiss my skin. I could see myself in the mirror opposite, only in a satin corset, nothing at all on the bottom, and I liked the effect, making a mental note to occasionally take my bottoms off first when dancing for customers. She was guiding my foot into the fetish pointe shoe – it was a tight fit, but after carefully unlacing and relacing, my foot found itself encased in the creation – and then the other one. The sensation was one you couldn't ignore; they were utterly uncomfortable in a way that made me aware of every part of my feet and legs, and they affected the angle of my pelvis even before I tried to stand. She helped me to my feet and I took a few careful steps, finding the point of balance.

'Very sexy, with no knickers,' she said, with a mocking note to her voice. 'Do you like the feeling of being restricted? Men like to see us like this, you know.'

'Not in my experience they don't. They always want to be on the receiving end of it.'

'You just haven't found the right person yet. Give me your hands.'

I held my hands out to her, intrigued. She took the other ballet shoes out of her bag and placed them on my hands, my fingers bending against the hard blocks in the toes, the leather still slightly warm from her feet. Where there was too much room at the heel she used the ribbons to secure them around my wrists, then, taking a roll of PVC bondage tape, she bound from the toes of the shoes to my elbow, wrapping tightly, till the shoe almost felt part of my hand, but left me with a blunt hoof instead of fingers, so I couldn't hold a drink, couldn't scratch an itch ... I'd also really struggle to remove them myself.

'Now, on all fours, use your pointes to walk on at the front.'

I bent over carefully and placed my hands on the ground, the ruthless pointe shoes forcing me to bend and spread my legs to keep my balance. She walked me around the changing room like a dog, holding on to my hair, with a practised touch which balanced severity and compassion. Knowing my bare arse and pussy were presented up to anyone who walked in made me wet, and all thoughts of everyday life were pushed from my head by the overload of physical sensations. She pulled my head around so I could see myself in the mirror, ran her hand down my back, and stroked a cold, slender finger over my pussy.

'You're all wet. I think you're ready to meet your man.'

I knew instantly she planned to make me go out into the club like this. I was slightly freaked out at the. Even for someone who gets naked for strangers every night, this was real exposure; my pussy was so wet everyone would be able to tell how aroused I was. I also worried the management might have something to say about it. But I'm not one who tries to control from the bottom; it takes a lot of trust and attraction to submit to someone, but once I do, I'm all theirs. I looked up at my mistress, and she held the door open for me as I crawled through.

All eyes were instantly on us. The hardened sex industry girls didn't bat an eyelid, the neon bikini brigade stared in disbelief, the customers looked on with a mixture of reactions which verged on confusion, except one, who looked on in pure lust. My ballerina mistress beckoned to him, a tall, well-built man in casual clothes but with a definite air of someone who's in charge at work, in life, and in the bedroom. She directed me into the private VIP room, a dark, velvety cocoon of a place, and I picked my way across the floor, my knuckles scuffing in my pointe shoes, painfully aware of the eyes on my dripping wet pussy.

They had a brief, hushed conversation and a huge amount of cash changed hands, which she stashed somewhere inside her rubber dress. She told me to get on the low table in the centre of the velvet couches, the wood hard against my knees but still some relief to be relieved of the bondage of walking on the shoes. I was so overwhelmed I just wanted to come, to release some of the tension that was built up in every bit of my body. I leant my chest forward onto the table and slid one hand between my legs. My pussy responded even though the PVC tape was rough and I craved the warm touch of skin on skin. Suddenly I felt a sharp sting across my buttocks, the blow just glancing my pussy so that I screamed out loud.

The man spoke for the first time. 'I don't remember telling you to touch yourself.'

I pleaded with him to finger my pussy, till he slapped my arse again.

'I'll decide when – if – you get my fingers. I think you should pleasure your beautiful mistress first.' He turned and addressed her. 'Would you like her to eat your pussy?'

She smiled, and manoeuvred herself onto the table in

front of me, pulling up her dress as she did so. Her panties were crotchless, and as she opened her legs I leant forward and pressed my lips to her pussy, opening my mouth slightly to part her lips and letting my tongue find her clit, her hands tangling in my hair as she pulled me closer. I've always had very sensitive lips, and on more than one occasion have orgasmed just from a good, long kiss, so tonguing and kissing her pussy was giving me as much pleasure as it was giving her. I thought about seeing her rip her tights open on stage and squirmed with pleasure at the thought that I was licking that same pussy. I knew she was coming and I concentrated on her clit, licking softly and rhythmically, her juices pooling on the table as she cried out.

'You're such a filthy bitch, look at the state of you. Naked from the waist down, cunt all wet, wearing fucked-up shoes, licking pussy, begging me to finger you.'

His hand landed again, I felt the burn, and it landed again, and again, on my buttocks, the backs of my thighs, and occasionally on my pussy, which hurt in the best possible way.

I heard him unclip his belt, and hardly had to wonder if he was going to tie mc up with it, or whether he was going to fuck me before the first lash of leather fell across the backs of my legs.

'Please, please fuck me,' I heard my own voice begging.

'Fuck yourself,' he sneered, lashing me with the belt again. I took it as permission, and ventured my hobbled hand in between my legs. I couldn't do much without freeing my fingers, but I was in such a heightened state, even the rough rubbing of the bound shoe was getting me off.

He laughed at my pathetic attempts. 'What do you think, has she been humiliated enough? Should I make her come?'

'It's up to you, darling,' she replied, lazing on the table in a post-orgasmic haze.

'I think so. I've got to be up in the morning, I can't be up all night playing with filthy sluts.'

His fingers ran up the backs of my legs, over the reddening skin, making it sting. He rubbed over my pussy once, making me gasp, then his finger rubbed my wetness over my arsehole to ease his finger inside. I screamed, my pussy gushing and the ache in my feet just serving to accentuate the pleasure. His finger slid in and out, till he pulled me onto my feet roughly, forcing me to balance on the shoes. I heard the rip of a condom packet and knew with relief he was finally going to fuck me. He was much bigger than me and held me easily as I wobbled on my fettered hands. I screamed as his cock slid easily into my arse and rubbed my clit with the leather pointe shoe, his hands gripping my hips as he pushed in and out. I came over and over again, as he insulted me, telling me in graphic detail how he could see his cock going into my arse and everyone could hear me screaming. The ballerina dominatrix watched intently for a while, her gaze simultaneously mocking and approving, till she seemed to get bored, counted out several hundred pounds (after keeping a generous cut for herself), and threw it on the table on front of me before walking out of the booth. Something in the sight of the money tipped me over the edge, knowing I was getting paid for one of the best sexual experiences I'd ever had, and I came again, clenching around his cock, catalyzing his orgasm, which I felt in the throbbing of his cock and his fingers biting into the flesh of my hips.

Thankfully, he proved to be a compassionate master, who untied my right hand before he left. On the walk of shame back to the dressing room I had more than my share of leery glances from dancers and customers.

* * *

I'm sore this morning. I can feel I've been really fucked, and my knuckles are grazed, my toes squashed and bruised. I've got a stack of cash, so I don't really need to work tonight. So why I've just texted the manager and booked myself in to work I'm not sure ...

Three's the Charm
by Elizabeth Coldwell

Someone told me not too long ago that the only difference between a wife and a prostitute is a wedding band. Now, you've probably heard that line before, but I never had, nor any one of a dozen similar comments, until I married Eddie Sorvino.

No one ever believes me when I say I didn't marry Eddie for his money. They look at me, with my blonde curls and my big tits and my lack of anything resembling a formal education. Then they look at him, with his balding head, his slight paunch, and his craggy, pockmarked face and they figure me to be nothing but a plain old gold-digger. But I love Eddie, I genuinely do. And I didn't know about his wealth when he first started coming into the coffee shop on 55th Street, where I was working as a waitress between mostly unsuccessful auditions for chorus work. In fact, there were a lot of things I didn't know about him, including his connections to the Mob. But I married him in spite of what might be generously called his murky past – and his equally murky present – and I've never regretted it for a moment.

You see, Eddie and I have a spectacular sex life, although that hasn't always been the case. When we first started dating, things were great. We'd slip between the sheets and I'd blow his dick till his eyes crossed. But it seemed as soon as that wedding ring went on my finger, it was like someone had thrown a bucket of iced water over Eddie's libido. Try as I might, I just couldn't get him in the mood. I tried dirty talk, using a big, black dildo on myself while he watched, turning up at his place of work wearing nothing but a garter belt and stockings under my coat. Nothing worked.

Now, if I really only had been interested in his money, a sexless marriage would have been fine by me. But I needed the physical side of things, and I needed them from Eddie. So I sat him down and got him to admit what was wrong.

It wasn't easy to get him to open up at first, but finally he told me all about it. Before he met me, Eddie used to visit hookers on a regular basis. It seemed he had tastes the women he'd dated weren't too keen on fulfilling, but working girls were only too happy to give him what he wanted. He hadn't tried asking me for anything too unusual, afraid that if he did, he'd scare me away. But, more than that, he actually liked the thrill he'd got from paying for sex.

I couldn't believe there would be many acts he could ask me to perform that I might refuse, once I'd established he didn't get off on toilet functions or anything likely to cause either of us lasting harm. And I hated the thought of him sneaking around and visiting hookers to get his pleasure, even though he swore he'd never so much as looked at another woman since we met. So I thought about it, and eventually I came up with a solution that suited us both. I would get the sex I craved and Eddie would be compensating me for it, though not with cash.

The charm bracelet beckoned to me every time I walked past the window of Morton's on Fifth Avenue. A simple silver band, it was designed to be filled up with charms representing important events in the wearer's life – or simply ones she found pretty. My plan was simple, and foolproof. Every time we had the kind of hot, nasty sex Eddie hankered after, he'd buy me a charm, and no one but us would ever know what they really signified.

The silver handbag, inlaid with rubies, is one of my very favourites. Eddie gave it to me the day after he fucked me in the arse for the first time. I'll never forget that night. He came home in really high spirits, for reasons he never quite explained – although I did wonder later whether it had anything to do with a former business associate of his, Tony Manetti, more usually known as Tony the Weasel, being found wearing concrete boots at the bottom of the Hudson River a couple of days later.

Whatever, it came as something of a surprise when Eddie cuddled up to me on the couch after dinner and started nuzzling my neck. It was the most attention he'd paid me in weeks, but I wasn't objecting.

As we kissed, he took my hand and placed it on the bulge in his pants. My pussy creamed at the feel of it, getting ready for the sex I'd been missing out on for so long. Eddie's next words threw me for a loop.

'Tina, baby, would you do something for me? Something a little bit – different.'

'Anything you want, you know that. You only have to ask.'

'Well, I – er …' He started fidgeting, unable to look me in the eye, and that's when I knew he was looking for something he'd previously only got from the hookers he visited.

'Come on, Eddie, spit it out. I'm not going to be upset.'

At last, he met my gaze. 'Tina, would you – would you let me fuck you in the arse?'

Now, I had to think about my answer for a moment. Even though I'd told him I wouldn't have a problem satisfying his kinkiest requests, Eddie was hung – and I mean really hung. I'd never seen anything that big outside of a porno, and I really wasn't sure I'd be able to take his thick chunk of meat in my tight little arsehole. But I was determined to do whatever it took to keep my Eddie happy, so finally I nodded and said, 'Sure.'

A grin lighting up his big, ugly face, Eddie scooped me into his arms and carried me through to the bedroom.

Dumping me down on the bed, he undid my pretty silk peignoir so he could kiss my bare, freckled tits. Getting between my legs, he ripped off my panties and buried his face in my snatch. He licked my clit for a while, getting me nice and juicy, then moved lower, so he could tongue my arsehole. It tickled a little, and I squirmed, partly in reaction to his eager rimming of my back door, and partly because I knew what would be taking the place of his tongue before long.

To make things easier for him, he took a bottle of lube out of the nightstand, the kind that's designed for anal play, which is when I figured he'd been planning this for a while, because he must have made a special trip out to get the supplies he needed. He greased up his trigger finger, then stuck it right up my hole. That felt so dirty, but kind of nice, and I wondered why none of his old flames had let him fuck their arse. Maybe, like me, they were worried about how he'd fit, or maybe they just thought nice girls didn't do that kind of thing. Well, I was starting to think I wasn't a nice girl, because my tummy was doing back flips at the thought of Eddie pulling out his finger and replacing it with his cock.

When he did, it didn't seem like he'd be able to get that huge tool inside me. He pushed and pushed, but nothing happened. Then I kind of pushed back at him, and to my surprise, the head of his dick popped inside me. He had to take his time getting the rest of his length up my arse, but once he'd filled me as full as he could, I felt so proud. My arsehole was stretched tight round his cock, and my whole pussy felt like it was quivering, my clit poking out from between my taut, wet lips. Eddie couldn't resist homing in on such an obvious target, and when he strummed it with his fingers, my cunt spasmed and I came so hard coloured lights danced before my eyes. The muscles in my arse nearly milked the come from him at that point, but Eddie's made of sterner stuff than that. While most other men would have shot their load just at the thought of finally getting inside their wife's virgin arsehole, he'd restrained himself through the whole process of opening me with his fingers and tongue, and he kept going even while I thrashed around in orgasm. He fucked me with slow, almost stately movements, just sawing in and out of my hole a little way, and only when I'd calmed down did he really start to fuck me hard. Of course, that just set me off again, like I'd never really come down from the peak of my first climax, and when I came a second time, it was with such force that I swear I actually passed out for a moment. Even a man with Eddie's fortitude couldn't resist the gripping, clutching motion of my arsehole this time, and he filled my bowels with all the hot, rich spunk he'd been saving up during our dry spell.

He dropped hot, grateful kisses on my lips, and I could have sworn there were tears in his eyes as he thanked me for letting him fuck my arse. When we finally pulled apart, I felt a definite soreness in my well-used hole, and I knew I'd pay the price for my exotic exertions. But even if I had to sit on a rubber ring for a couple of days, the wonderful sex I'd shared with Eddie had been more than worth it. And I had our trip to Morton's to look forward to, where my husband would treat me to that gorgeous handbag charm as a very special thank you for making one of his most cherished desires come true.

The next charm Eddie bought for me was the purple enamelled daisy. I got that the day after I spanked his arse with a ping pong bat for being a naughty boy. When he outlined that little fantasy to me, I must admit I was a bit surprised. It didn't seem to fit the image I had of my strong, powerful husband as a man who took no shit and most definitely didn't like to be ridiculed. The last guy who called Eddie a pussy to his face, Lucky Johnny Vitale, lost most of the fingers on his left hand in what the police report described as a "gardening accident", even though everyone knew Lucky Johnny had never done a day's gardening in his life. So when Eddie told me about all the verbal humiliation he wanted me to put him through, I really wasn't too sure I wanted to go down that path. But he assured me he would never hurt a hair on my head, and that sometimes a man who was very powerful and dominant in his working life needed the satisfaction that came from being bossed around in the bedroom.

So I put all my misgivings to one side, and dressed up the way he asked me to, in a tight-fitting skirt, a blouse that strained to contain my tits, fishnet stockings and some horn-rimmed glasses Eddie found in a junk shop, that didn't actually have any glass in the lenses. I looked like a slutty school teacher, but that was just the effect Eddie was hoping for, and from the way his cock stood to attention in his pinstriped pants I knew he was turned on to the point where he couldn't stand it. I'd happily have dropped my panties and let him fuck me where I stood, but he wanted his punishment first. So I walked round him as he stood there with his head bowed, slapping that bat against my palm and telling him what a bad boy he was, and how he wasn't fit to lick the soles of my shoes. The only thing what would make him learn his lesson, I said, was to have his arse paddled till it was red and sore, and he didn't argue with me once, just kept saying, 'Yes, ma'am,' and, 'I promise I won't do it again, ma'am.'

To my surprise, I was getting really horny just thinking of the moment when he'd have to drop his pants and present his bare butt to me, ready to be punished. My panties were soaking wet, clinging to my freshly shaved cunt lips, and I had to fight the urge to drop a finger between my thighs and finger my needy puss. With all the self-restraint I could muster, I ordered Eddie to bend over for his much-needed spanking. He didn't argue, just undid his fly buttons so his pants slithered down to his knees, and got into position.

If only his pals could see him now, I thought, stalking round him and building up the sense of anticipation. Hell, if the cops in the local precinct knew I'd got him like this, waiting meek as a lamb to have his arse thrashed, they'd probably bust a gut laughing. But this wasn't about the cops, or Eddie's Mob buddies, or anyone but the two of us. He'd asked for this particular pleasure, and I was only too happy to make his wishes come true.

I gave him a couple of swats through his underwear, not too hard at first as, stupid as this might sound, I didn't want to hurt him. Eddie begged me to put more force into the blows, and once I'd realised he was getting off on me pounding his butt, I gave him everything I'd got. After a dozen slaps, I peeled his briefs down, curious to see what kind of pain I'd inflicted. His skin looked red and blotchy as raw hamburger, and was hot to the touch when I ran a fingertip over it, but still he wanted more. So I whacked him another 12 or so times on his bare arse.

By now, I'd really begun to enjoy myself, strutting round him between swats, telling him what a miserable little son of a bitch he was, and how all the jewellery in Morton's couldn't even begin to compensate me for having to thrash some sense into him. Eddie was clearly loving this, even though his butt cheeks were bright flaming scarlet, and he kept calling me the best wife any guy could have.

When I finally dropped the paddle, Eddie's dick was as hard as I'd ever known it, even though he must have been in agony from his spanking. I soothed his sore arse with plenty of aloe moisturising cream, smoothing it into his punished skin, then I got down on my knees – hard as that was in my skin-tight pencil skirt – and sucked his cock like I'd never get enough of it. As I gazed up at my beloved husband, cheeks hollowed from the power of my suction and my 40 bucks a tube lipstick smeared all along his thick, gnarled shaft, I knew these spanking games were destined to become a regular part of our life.

And the next day Eddie presented me with the daisy charm.

But my very favourite charm, and the one that brings back the fondest memories of the night I earned it, is the silver heart with a small pink diamond set in it. Eddie was even more sheepish than usual about approaching me with his request, and after much stuttering and stammering he admitted he wanted to see me in action with another man.

'This is going to sound odd, I know, Tina,' he said, 'but the thought of you with some big stud's cock in your mouth or your cute little pussy gets me harder than anything else.'

'And do you have any particular big stud in mind?' I asked.

'Well, I – er – I was kind of talking to Pauly de Vito over a couple of drinks at Mancini's the other night, and I offered him first refusal.'

'You what?' In truth, I was nowhere near as mad at him as I made out. Pauly was something in the import and export business, as handsome as Eddie was ugly, with thick, black hair he always wore gelled back from his face and a muscular build beneath his hand-tailored Italian suits. Rumour had it he was nearly as well hung as Eddie, and the thought of being fucked by him while Eddie looked on had my pussy flowing like the Hudson. I didn't need any kind of bribe to act out this little fantasy, but Eddie didn't need to know that.

'I'm sorry, baby, I know I should have spoken to you about this first, but –'

Putting a finger to Eddie's lips, I shushed away his apology. 'It's OK. You know I'll do this for you.'

'Great, because I've invited Pauly over for cocktails tomorrow night.'

That gave me time to have my hair done, have my bikini line waxed smooth and treat myself to a new set of black lacy lingerie – all on Eddie's credit card, of course. I knew he'd want me to look as desirable as possible for Pauly's arrival, and he wouldn't mind in the least paying for it.

Pauly arrived at seven the next evening, bearing a bottle of vintage Champagne and a dozen red roses. Charm oozed from him as he kissed me on the doorstep, complimenting me on my beauty in Italian. As I led him through to the living room, a thought popped into my mind. Had Eddie offered me to the man as a sweetener for one of his business deals? I didn't know and I didn't care. All I could think of in my lust-dazed state was the moment when Pauly's pants would come down and I learnt whether the rumours were true.

Eddie mixed Martinis for the three of us, skewering olives on cocktail sticks and dropping them into the finished drinks. As the three of us sat there, Pauly and Eddie discussing mutual acquaintances and the fate of the unfortunate Tony the Weasel, me listening with only half an ear, it could have passed for any normal social occasion at our home. Only the rising sexual tension in the air, fuelled by the sneaky peeks Pauly was taking at my long, smooth legs where they emerged from the hem of my little black dress and the suggestive way I munched on my cocktail olive in return, gave any clue that we would soon be progressing to the bedroom.

A CD was playing in the background – Frank Sinatra, my husband's all-time hero – and Eddie murmured, 'Pauly, why don't you ask Tina to dance?'

'Sure thing.' Pauly set down his empty glass and held out a hand, asking gruffly, 'Princess, would you care to dance?'

I'd hardly call what we did over the next few minutes dancing. Pauly held me so close I could feel his dick pressing hard at my lower belly, and with his hands on my arse cheeks, he ground himself into me in time to the music. Glancing over at Eddie, I checked his reaction to our blatant dry-humping. He couldn't take his eyes off us, and when Pauly unzipped my dress, letting it slither to the floor, Eddie freed his hugely swollen cock from his pants and stroked it in time to the music.

My tiny lace thong followed, leaving me in just a half-cup bra and my heels, and Pauly feasted on that sight while he stripped out of his own clothes. His cock wasn't a monster like Eddie's, but it was thick, with beads of precome already dripping from its tip. Without ceremony, Pauly sat me back on the couch, raising my legs in the air so he could get between them and start ploughing me. It was the kind of position you only see in pornos, but I felt like a porn star at that moment, putting on a never-to-be-forgotten performance for our audience of one. Eddie's hand moved faster on his dick as he watched Pauly shoving all the way into me before pulling right out again, fucking me with measured strokes. His cock was hitting the spot on my inner walls that, if you touch it just right, can make me come without me needing to stroke my clit, and I knew my orgasm wasn't far off. When it arrived, I may have shrieked a little louder than usual, leaving Eddie in no doubt I'd hit my peak, and letting Pauly know he had the magic touch.

Pauly was a long way off coming, and I hoped he'd take me over the edge a couple more times before he finally did. Not wanting my husband to be left out of what was shaping up to be one of the best fucks of my life, I beckoned him over. Closing my lips round the head of his cock, I let him push as deep into my mouth as he could. I'd never had two men at once before, and the three of us felt connected by a strong current of sexual energy that flowed through me, stoked with every synchronised thrust of the dicks in my mouth and pussy.

When I came for a second time, it felt as though I'd never stop. Eddie followed quickly, shooting his tangy load down my throat and murmuring sweet words of love and gratitude for pleasing his associate as well as him. Pauly's climax was longer, more drawn out, and when I'd milked all of his outpouring from him, he praised me on having the most skilled cunt he'd ever known.

'She's got heart too,' Eddie told him, making a reference

to my longed-for charm that only I would understand, leaving Pauly to ponder why we couldn't stop laughing as we held each other tight.

It's our wedding anniversary next week, and I have the feeling Eddie's going to ask me to live out another of his fantasies to celebrate the occasion. I don't know what he has in mind, only that the sex will be mind-blowing and he'll present me with another addition to my bracelet as a show of his appreciation. Our little arrangement might not be to everyone's tastes, but I truly am living a charmed life.